"You'd do that for me?" Eva asked incredulously.

She stared at him and continued, "You'd ask family friends to take me in?"

Brooks nodded. "It wouldn't be the first time I've asked the Chatam sisters to take in a pa— er, person."

"No? What other *patients* have you asked these sisters to take in?" she asked, grinning at him.

Brooks looked her straight in the eye. "You know I can't tell you that."

Eva grinned and swayed toward him, her long pale hair glimmering. He had to admit that he'd never seen a more exotic, graceful, breathtaking sight. He hoped that she would refuse so he could wash his hands of her.

She did not.

"Okay. I guess I can stand a little antebellum mansion. Just until I can figure out what to do next."

He gulped, disappointed and strangely pleased. "Let's go then." He walked her to the car, without releasing her arm, and handed her down into it.

He was bringing his best friend's aunties another foundling, and he hoped that she wasn't going to break all their hearts.

Arlene James has been publishing steadily for nearly four decades and is a charter member of RWA. She is married to an acclaimed artist, and together they have traveled extensively. After growing up in Oklahoma, Arlene lived thirty-four years in Texas and now abides in beautiful northwest Arkansas, near two of the world's three loveliest, smartest, most talented granddaughters. She is heavily involved in her family, church and community.

Books by Arlene James

Love Inspired

Chatam House

Anna Meets Her Match
A Match Made in Texas
Baby Makes a Match
An Unlikely Match
Second Chance Match
Building a Perfect Match
His Ideal Match
The Bachelor Meets His Match
The Doctor's Perfect Match

Eden, OK

His Small-Town Girl
Her Small-Town Hero
Their Small-Town Love

Visit the Author Profile page at Harlequin.com for more titles.

The Doctor's Perfect Match

Arlene James

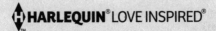

Recycling programs
for this product may
not exist in your area.

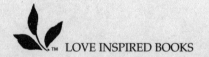 LOVE INSPIRED BOOKS

ISBN-13: 978-0-373-81848-8

The Doctor's Perfect Match

www.Harlequin.com

Printed in U.S.A.

Be joyful in hope, patient in affliction,
faithful in prayer.
—*Romans* 12:12

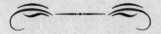

For Erica,
who has made my son so very happy
and his mom forever grateful.

Chapter One

Even in Buffalo Creek, Texas, with the bright sunshine streaming down and the utter absence of wind, January meant chill temperatures. Still, the willowy blonde had found a unique way to gather a crowd for her sales demonstration. Beneath the awning that she'd erected beside her minivan, she chattered and joked, flipping her long, straight butter-yellow hair, winking her big catlike eyes at her laughing onlookers, the colorful scarves draped about her person waving languidly. All the while she worked, she pressed bits of string and wood, gravel and broken glass into a damp clay disk, which she would presumably then bake in a small microwave oven at her elbow.

As tired as he was, Dr. Brooks Leland would have liked to have paused and joined in the fun, but he'd promised his best friend, Morgan, that he wouldn't be late to dinner. For once. Besides, since the untimely death of his pretty blonde wife, he avoided women—especially blondes—like the plague. Oh, he would do it again, go through all the pain and the grief, just for those two short years with Brigitte. He would not, however, risk that kind of loss for anyone else, let alone stand in the cold just to watch a lovely woman try to sell unusual objects of art created on the spot.

Hurrying past the crowd, he crossed the parking lot to the entrance of the grocery store. Once inside, he picked up the multigrain bread requested by his hostess and, on impulse, grabbed a bouquet of flowers.

He'd given up trying to make his old buddy jealous. Not that he'd ever had any real interest in Lyla Simone anyway, but it had taken a mighty shove to make the confirmed bachelor professor tumble into love with his comely graduate student, and Brooks had been only too glad to deliver the blow. Once he'd fallen, Morgan Chatam had fallen hard. He was not a man to give his heart lightly, as Brooks understood all too well. It did Brooks's heart good to see his old friend so happy after all these years, and for that reason alone he would take Lyla Simone flowers forever. The joy of having a goddaughter—Lyla and Morgan's child—suddenly thrust into his life only gave him more cause. They'd named her Brigitte Kay, after Brooks's late wife and one of Morgan's aunts. She was an adorable little thing, happily and unabashedly spoiled, and in truth, she was the one thing Brooks envied his old friend.

Brooks made it through the checkout line, but before he could take his change, a teenaged male by the name of Jason Crowel burst inside, yelling for him.

"Doc Leland! Doc Leland! She fell down, and blood's all over!"

Leaving everything behind, Brooks bolted for the door. He saw the crowd as soon as he hit the parking lot. Brooks sighed inwardly. It *would* be the blonde. Jason caught up to him, bouquet and grocery bag clutched in his hands. The sides of Brooks's overcoat flapped like wings as he sprinted across the pavement. Digging into the pockets of his dark slacks, he found his car keys and plucked them out as he drew near the van, Jason at his heels. He set off the car alarm so the young man knew which car to go to, then tossed the keys to Jason.

"Leave the groceries and flowers, grab the medical bag off the backseat."

"Yessir."

Elbowing his way into the crowd, Brooks asked, "What's happened here?"

Several people began speaking at the same time.

"She started talking gibberish and just toppled over."

"Hit her head on the pavement before anyone could catch her."

"Splattered blood all over."

The woman sat up, blinking at Brooks in confusion, blood streaking her pale hair. He checked her pulse, which was rapid and erratic, while speaking in a calm, reassuring tone.

"I'm Dr. Brooks Leland. You've taken a nasty blow to the head. Try not to move. Can you tell me your name?"

She lifted a hand toward her head. He caught it and gently pushed it down again, repeating his question.

"Can you tell me your name?"

"Tharestershestersaben," she babbled.

Jason returned with the medical bag, and Brooks took out his penlight, instructing firmly, "If no one has already done so, please call an ambulance."

He made a quick examination, determined that her pupils were unequally reactive and that she needed stitches in her scalp, at the very least. Moreover, she seemed painfully thin, despite a suspiciously shapely figure beneath a heavy black leotard and all those artfully draped scarves. After applying a compress to staunch the flow of blood from the laceration to her scalp, he glanced around him.

"Any idea who she is?"

Murmurs of denial went through the crowd

before someone said, "License plate on the van is Missouri."

Not a local girl, then, though even with Texas license plates, she might not be known. Texas was a big state, and the eight-million-strong Dallas-Fort Worth metroplex sprawled just thirty-five miles to the north of Buffalo Creek, which itself boasted some twenty thousand souls.

The ambulance arrived within five minutes, but in that time he managed to stop the bleeding from the scalp wound. His patient remained remarkably composed, though she said not a single coherent word. He suspected a stroke and feared that she might be bleeding inside her skull. He made a phone call.

"Morgan, I'm afraid I'm going to be late for dinner, after all."

Eva recognized the tap-tap-tap of typing even before she opened her eyes. The room swam for a moment, refusing to come into focus and seeming much too bright. She automatically lifted a hand to shield her eyes, which ached with a ferocity that alarmed but also reassured her.

The light flickered out just as a pleasantly masculine voice said, "Welcome back. You've been sedated."

She remembered all too well struggling to get up off the X-ray table and telling them over and over again that she categorically refused to have pictures made of her head, but of course they hadn't understood a word she'd been saying. Still, the sedation had been a dirty trick. Reminding herself that they had merely been trying to help, she cleared her throat, swallowed and attempted to speak.

"That's a relief." The greater relief was that the words had come out clearly. Flush with success, she quipped, "For a minute I thought it was one of those deals where I'd had so much fun I'd forgotten."

"Your speech has cleared. You experienced expressive aphasia. That's a condition where—"

"My brain was speaking English, but my tongue was talking Martian. Yeah, I got that."

"Is your head hurting?"

"On a scale of one to ten, if a plastic doll is a one and Marilyn Monroe in her prime is a ten, let's go with Marilyn," she gritted out, gingerly fingering the heavy bandage on the back of her head. At the same time, she realized that most of her clothes were gone, replaced by a hospital gown, though she still wore her leggings and socks. "So did I crack the bone?"

"Just your scalp, thankfully."

"How many stitches did I wind up with?"

"About twenty."

"Yowza. Did they have to shave my head?"

"We did," he answered.

"But your hair's so thick it will cover up the

bald spot nicely," said a reassuring female voice. At the same time, movement to Eva's left drew her attention to a nurse adjusting the drip on a saline bag.

"That's good," she muttered. Wouldn't want to leave an ugly corpse.

"You almost certainly have a concussion," the doctor went on smoothly. "Your pupils are not equally reactive. I really did not want to have to sedate you."

The nurse added, "You gave us no other option. Doctor hasn't left your side since, though."

Eva closed her eyes and carefully turned her head in his direction, gasping despite her best efforts to deny the pain. "It's the ICP," she murmured.

"Intracranial pressure," he said. "Yes, that would be my guess. Are you a medical professional? You seem familiar with the terminology."

"Worked as a transcriptionist."

"I see. Well, I've already administered IV medication that will reduce the swelling," he told her, "and now that you're awake, I can give you something to help with the pain. Are you allergic to any drugs?"

"Nope. None I've ever tried, that is. Hey, that's not a confession, by the way, just in case you're a DEA agent in deep cover."

She heard him chuckle as he tapped. Then he moved around, supposedly injecting something into the IV line as he spoke. "Not a DEA agent. Just a doctor. That should take effect soon."

"Not soon enough."

"I've ordered an EEG, and—"

"No," she said.

"An EEG will tell us—"

"It won't tell you anything of significance," she said, forcing open her eyes.

After the first flash of pain, her vision cleared and the pounding inside her skull settled to a survivable throb. He was even more handsome than she remembered, ridiculously so. She tried to focus on the black slacks, white shirt and black tie worn beneath an immaculately white lab coat, but she couldn't ignore the tall, fit, broad-shouldered man inside them.

Coal black hair brushed straight back from a high forehead with strokes of silver at the temples looked very distinguished on a square-jawed face. A perfect nose, wide, spare mouth that showed a decided tendency to smile and a healthy tan added up to the ideal masculine blend. The eyes were what did it, though. Tawny-gold to go with the silver streaks, they all but shouted, "Treasure! This man is a treasure!" They declared his intelligence and a depth of character that seemed out of place in a man well shy of fifty. She'd be surprised, in fact, if he was much past forty, despite the threads of sliver at his temples.

Regardless of those eyes and all they proclaimed, she frowned. She disliked handsome men on principle, especially those who knew they were handsome. And he knew it. As if challenging her to deny it, he grinned, displaying rascally dimples, a double set, twin grooves that slashed deeply into his cheeks on either side of his mouth and bracketed his even, white smile.

Turning away from the computer terminal mounted on the wall beside the bed, he pulled over a rolling stool with his foot and sat. He was a tall one; at least three inches over six feet, she judged. Being a tall woman—five feet nine-inches—she appreciated a tall man, especially one tall enough that she didn't have to wear flats as a sop to his vanity. She liked heels, spike heels that showed off her long legs, not that it mattered anymore. Not much did.

"I introduced myself before," he said, putting out a square-palmed, long-fingered hand, "but it may need repeating. Dr. Brooks Leland. I was in the grocery store when you collapsed."

"Lucky me," she said, shaking his hand.

"If you believe in luck," he returned, inclining his head.

"You don't?"

"No."

She lifted an eyebrow, her hand still in his. "What, then? Fate?"

"No. And you still haven't told me your name."

The medication was beginning to work and

work well, so she inched closer, as if prepared to confide in him. "Don't you know that all the most attractive women are mysterious by nature?" she whispered. The nurse snorted and tried to cover it with a cough.

He bent closer still and said, "The most attractive women eat healthy diets. When was the last time *you* ate?"

As if to remind her that it had been far too long, her stomach rumbled loudly. She hid her embarrassment behind a sultry smile and a smoky tone of voice. "Complaining about my figure, Doc?" she asked, squeezing his hand.

He let go of her, sat back and said to the nurse, "Bring her a full meal tray, please. Right away."

"Yes, Doctor."

The nurse swept instantly from the room, his word apparently being law.

The door hadn't bumped closed before he leaned his elbows on the bed rail, looked down at Eva and bluntly stated, "The breast implants do not hide the fact that you are much too thin. I don't see signs of bulimia or anorexia, so I have to conclude that you simply haven't been able to eat regularly. Now, I ask you again, when was the last time you ate?"

She sighed and looked at the peaks of her toes beneath the blanket. "It's been a day or two." She could feel his unrelenting gaze boring into her. "Okay, it was day before yesterday."

"Because?"

"Duh. Do you have any idea how difficult it is to get good caviar?" she cracked sarcastically. When he didn't laugh, she added, "I'm broke, all right?"

Her money had been running short even before the van had broken down. Thankfully, they'd gassed it after making the repairs in Lancaster. Considering what they'd charged her, they should have done that and more. She'd be out of here shortly, though where she'd go she had no idea. The old jalopy ought to have enough juice to get her to Waco, though.

"That explains the art show in January," the doctor muttered.

A male technician pushed a cart into the room just then, announcing, "EEG."

"I've already told you, no EEG," Eva insisted.

"Why not?" Dr. Leland wanted to know. "The machine's already here. Doesn't take long. You can be done before your dinner arrives."

"What part of broke don't you get?" she demanded, rolling her eyes at him. "I can't afford it. Okay? Besides, it's not going to tell you diddly. Anyone who knows me can attest that my brain function has never been normal. Trust me."

"And where would I find these people who can attest to your abnormal brain function?" he asked lightly.

She opened her mouth to tell him, realizing

only at the last moment what she'd be giving away. "Ah, ah, ah," she scolded, wagging a finger. "I hate to stiff you, Doc. I really do. But a billing address won't do you a bit of good. You can't get blood out of a turnip, as the saying goes. Besides, I didn't ask to be brought here."

He just smiled. "You weren't in any condition to ask, and this hospital takes all patients, regardless of their ability to pay."

"Oh. Cool. Well, I'm on my way out of here as soon as I eat and change, anyway. I appreciate the tailoring." She waved a hand at the bandage. "But I've got places to go, Doc, things to do."

He held up his hands, waved away the technician and said, "I'll cancel the order."

The tech shrugged and wheeled the cart out of the room.

"You are a very stubborn young lady," he said, getting up and going back to the computer.

"Thank you!" she chirped, grinning. "I haven't been called a young lady in ages."

He chuckled. "Just how old are you anyway?"

She didn't see any reason not to tell him. "Thirty-four."

"You look younger."

"Sweet. How old are you?"

He didn't hesitate. "Forty-four."

That, she decided, worked perfectly. "You look forty-four."

He laughed. "Thanks. I think."

"What's wrong with looking forty-four if you are forty-four?" she asked. "Especially if you're a gorgeous forty-four."

There was something freeing about losing the ability to filter what you said, freeing and frightening. Dr. Leland cleared his throat and said nothing, just pecked away at the computer keyboard. He finished and went out. A few minutes later, her meal arrived.

It consisted of a cold sandwich, a bag of chips, a banana, a cup of gelatin, a piece of carrot cake and a carton of milk. She chugged the milk and ate the cake, then went after the gelatin, saving the banana, chips and sandwich for later. Just a few minutes after pledging to save the banana for breakfast, though, she scarfed that down, too. She'd just laid aside the peel, feeling pleasantly stuffed, when Dr. Leland walked back into the room, accompanied by the nurse.

He glanced knowingly at the wrapped sandwich and chips cradled in her lap but said only, "I have some papers for you to sign."

"Sure," she agreed happily.

He produced the papers, a pen and a clipboard. She scrawled. He studied. After a moment, he lifted an eyebrow at her.

"Calamity Jane?"

She just shrugged, grinning. She should have known that if anyone could decipher her purposefully illegible penmanship, it would be a doctor.

"All right, Calamity, let's have a look."

The nurse turned on the overhead light. Eva smiled to let him know that the twinge of pain she felt was entirely manageable. While he listened to her heart, the nurse took a blood pressure cuff from a wire basket on the wall and wrapped it around Eva's upper arm. Then she took Eva's blood pressure while he checked her pupils. Next, he let down the side of the bed, took her by the wrist and had her sit up, swing her legs to the side and eventually stand. Finally he had her walk around. She felt perfectly steady on her feet, and while her head throbbed, it wasn't fierce.

Holding up the sandwich and the bag of chips, she looked back over her shoulder at him and said, "Guess I shouldn't skip quite so many meals, huh?"

He sent her an implacable look, saying nothing. Then he reached behind him and snagged a plastic bag from a chair against the wall.

Tossing the bag onto the foot of the bed, he said, "Get dressed. When you're ready, I'll drive you back to your vehicle."

"Yea!" she exclaimed in a small, comical voice. "Or put another way…" She inclined her head regally, feeling just a twinge of pain. "Thank you for your hospitality, but I really must be going now."

Shaking his head, he left the room again, opening the door for the nurse to leave ahead of him. Eva's relief evaporated instantly. Sighing, she plopped down on the foot of the bed, with all that currently stood between her and starvation clutched to her chest. She looked at the cold wrapped sandwich in one hand and the bag of chips in the other then tossed them onto the pillow. What did it matter? What did any of it matter?

For a moment she entertained the notion of staying where she was and letting that too-handsome doctor tend her. But, no, she couldn't do that. Eventually he'd figure out who she was and, if she couldn't prevent it, how to contact those she'd left behind, which meant that Ricky would be put through the same horrific ordeal that she'd had to endure. *That* she could not allow.

Nope, better just to carry on to the bitter end. She'd heard there were some lovely spots in south Texas where she could winter. She'd get some money together, find a remote place where she could hide. With luck they wouldn't find her until spring or even summer. By then Ricky would be well adjusted to her absence. Poor kid. He'd had some tough breaks, but this was the best of a bad lot of options that she could see. She hoped he could forgive her, but if not, so be it.

Shoving aside such maudlin thoughts, she got dressed. After pulling her black long-sleeved knit top over her head, she tied three shawls about her waist to make a skirt then draped a triangular scarf diagonally over one shoulder and knotted that at her waist. A second scarf went over the opposite shoulder, crisscrossing the other. She tied a third about her neck and tucked the point into the waistband of her leggings, letting the top drape loosely. Stacking up the final three colorful, silky shawls, she tossed them about her shoulders. They were amazingly warm, as generations of women throughout history well knew.

Her leather clogs were in the bottom of the bag with her cell phone. She dropped them to the floor and slipped her feet into them, adding over two inches to her height.

Taking the plastic bag, she dropped the sandwich and the chips into it. Then she helped herself to a pair of latex gloves and a small box of tissues on the counter before sitting down on the edge of the bed to wait. Barely had she parked herself before a knock sounded lightly, and the door cracked open.

"Are you decent?"

"Well, I'm dressed," she drawled. "Beyond that I make no promises."

Dr. Leland backed into the room, wearing a suit beneath a long overcoat and rolling a wheelchair behind him. "What are you, a stand-up comedienne?"

"If the shoe fits," she retorted cheerfully, holding up one foot.

"Ha-ha."

She eyed the wheelchair reluctantly. "Do I really need that?"

"Depends. Do you want to walk back to that grocery store parking lot or ride?"

Sighing melodramatically, she got up and plopped down in the wheelchair. "And you say *I'm* stubborn."

"If the *other* shoe fits..."

"Well, we know *you* are no stand-up comedian," she quipped.

He rolled her out of the room. As they moved through the area, Eva couldn't help noticing that nurses rushed to open doors, move carts and just generally smooth the way, always flashing smiles and coy looks at the doctor. Eva could stand it just so long before waving her arms and singing at the top of her lungs, "Hel-lo! Patient coming through. Doctor Luscious is just half the parade."

"Will you behave?" he growled. "Or can you not help yourself?"

"Why should I?"

Then again, why shouldn't she? After all, what did she care if all the nurses in the hospital cast lures at the man? He was someone else's problem. Poor woman. She probably didn't have a moment's peace. Of course there would be someone, probably several someones. A man as good-looking as he, and a doctor no less, could have his pick. He could even be married, though she had noticed no wedding ring—and hated that she had noticed. Apparently impending doom did not produce wisdom any more than did hard experience.

He wheeled her through a waiting room and then a pair of automatic glass doors onto a covered sidewalk. A luxury sedan sat waiting at the curb. A uniformed security guard, female, slid out from behind the steering wheel and walked around to take the chair after Eva vacated it. Leland opened the passenger door for Eva, kissed the security guard on the cheek, reducing the hefty woman to giggles, and rushed around the front of the car to the driver's side, his overcoat flapping with the force of his strides.

Eva was buckling up when he dropped down behind the steering wheel. He followed suit, tossed a wave at the still-tittering security guard and put the car in gear. Eva shook her head.

"You have no shame, do you?"

"What on earth are you talking about?"

"You kissed the security guard! It's not enough the nurses are all in love with you? You *must* have the security guard, too?"

He rolled his eyes. "For your information, she's family."

Eva blinked at that. "Oh. Well, in my defense, everyone's wrong sometimes."

Starting the engine, he shook his head. "She's my late wife's cousin, actually, and she's married. And she has two grown children. And her husband is disabled."

Those two words, *late wife*, rang inside Eva's

skull like a bell, reverberating repeatedly. *Late wife, late wife, late wife...*

"All right already," Eva cried melodramatically. "I was wrong. So shoot me."

"I'm just saying." He hunched his shoulders.

Eva trained her gaze on the scenery passing by her window. Okay, she conceded silently, so he really was rather likable, when he wasn't being all handsome and knowing and authoritative.

Several minutes passed before he spoke again. "And the nurses are not all in love with me. Actually, none of them are in love with me."

She chanced a glance at him and found him scowling. "How do you know?"

"I just do."

"O-kay." A smile almost surprised her. She had to work at keeping it away. She got very interested in the scenery again.

A few minutes later he said, "You'll need to have those stitches removed in about a week."

"Will do."

He pulled an envelope from inside his coat and tossed it into her lap. "Give that to the doctor who does it."

She looked at the envelope but not at him. "All righty."

Shifting in his seat, he added, "I suggest you get a good night's sleep before you drive."

Turning back to the window, she gave him a noncommittal answer. "Very well."

After a few more blocks, he said, "Don't throw that envelope away."

"I won't."

"I mean it."

She finally looked at him again. "I said I wouldn't. What's with you?"

"I tucked a few bucks in there, if that's all right with you," he snapped. Then, more mildly, he added, "You said you were broke."

"Oh." Surprised and truly chastened, she looked down at the envelope. "That's very kind. Thank you."

"No problem," he muttered, staring straight ahead.

A few seconds later the comfortable car turned into the grocery store parking lot and stopped.

Eva looked around. So did Leland. Then they looked at each other.

"Uh-oh," he said.

She chose a more colorful word. "Crud."

Her van was gone.

Chapter Two

"There were only four payments left!" Eva Belle Russell squawked. "And I just had it repaired."

Brooks dropped the small cell phone into his coat pocket, sighing deeply. "According to the police, you were four payments behind. They had no choice but to impound the vehicle."

What a mess. At least he had learned her name and that the vehicle had been financed through a bank in the Kansas City area, though what good that information did him, he wasn't sure, especially if she continued to refuse treatment.

"Well," she drawled, employing that broad wit of hers, "my aunt always said I'd wind up a street-walker. Looks like she was right. Literally."

She reached for the door handle, but of course he couldn't let her just get out and walk away, not in her condition. Objecting would undoubtedly cost him, though; in fact, he had to *make* himself do it. She actually got the door open and one foot out before he could speak.

"Eva, wait."

She looked around at him. "Got my name, did you?"

"Eva Belle Russell."

She wilted, sinking back into the seat as if defeated by the simple fact of being known. "What are you going to do?" she asked warily.

"Depends. How much trouble are you in?"

Some of her spunk returned. "My head's cracked. I'm broke. I'm stranded. My car's been repossessed! Is that enough for you?"

"Are you in *legal* trouble?" he demanded.

"No!" She folded her arms, muttering, "Other than the repossession thing. And I guess that's taken care of now."

"I mean, *criminal* trouble," he clarified.

She gaped at him. "You think I'd be going without meals if I didn't have scruples?"

That made a certain sense. A criminal would have simply shoplifted her next meal or walked out on an unpaid bill. He supposed the threat of repossession could be reason enough to want to keep her identity a secret, though with the original license plate hanging out there for all the world to see, such secrecy felt pointless. On the other hand, given her physical condition, who was to say that she was even thinking clearly? He wished she'd let him take the EEG. That, however, was not the immediate problem.

"Is there anyone you can call?" He knew she had a cell phone on her and that it contained no preprogrammed numbers and not one iota of personal information.

"No."

"Where are you headed? Maybe I can take you there."

She pulled in a deep breath. "Um, what's the next town of any size down the road? Waco?"

Obviously she had no real destination in mind. The woman was a gypsy, a free spirit, peddling her artwork wherever she could. A free spirit with very real problems.

"I'll take you back to the hospital."

"Forget that." She shook her head, rippling her blond locks and making her eyeballs roll with pain so that she clasped the bandage beneath her hair gingerly.

"Look," he said, tiring of the game, the situation and the whole endless day. "I know about the brain tumor. We did a non-contrast CT while you were unconscious. It's standard proce—"

She all but leaped out of the car. It was nearly dark and the middle of January, but the fool woman actually got out of the car and headed off as if she had someplace to go.

"Eva!"

"Thanks, Doc. I've had fun. So long, now."

"Eva Belle Russell," he hollered, at the end of his tether, "you get back in this car!"

She walked off toward the grocery store. Grinding his teeth, Brooks got out and went after her.

"Where do you think you're going?"

"Where it's warm."

"You can't sleep in the grocery store."

She swirled in a circle, her scarves whirling around her, but she kept walking. "I'll have you know that I once slept all night in a lawn chair. I'll be fine."

"The grocery store closes at ten."

She lifted both hands. "You must have a homeless shelter around here somewhere."

They did, but they wouldn't take her with that bandage on the back of her head. She might sneak it past them, but he doubted it. Besides, she belonged in a hospital, at least until he knew exactly with what she was dealing.

"Have you ever spent the night in a homeless shelter?" he demanded, stopping in his tracks.

She stopped, too, and turned to face him. "I'm not going back to the hospital."

"Do you even know what type of tumor it is?"

"Oligodendroglioma."

Not good, but not necessarily fatal, and he

noted that the medical term rolled off her tongue with the ease of familiarity.

"Temporal, obviously," he noted to himself. "Grade?"

"Three."

"For sure?"

"Sure enough."

"Anaplastic?"

"I haven't had a biopsy, but it's assumed."

"Other than the language issues, which are transient, and some impulse control, are you having any other symptoms? Seizures, perhaps?"

She shrugged.

Exasperated, he demanded, "How can you not know if you're having seizures?"

She parked her hands at her waist. "Well, I haven't exactly been eating regularly, as you've pointed out."

The anger caught him entirely off guard. "In other words, you don't know if you've been getting dizzy and passing out from hunger or from seizures?" She shrugged again, and it was all he could do not to shake her by her too slender shoulders. "You *belong* in a hospital."

"I'm *not going* to the hospital," she stated flatly. Then she added in a silly singsong, "and you can't make me." She actually stuck out her tongue.

He didn't know whether to laugh or tear out his hair, so he did neither, instead saying with admirable coolness, "I won't dignify that with a reply. Just tell me why you won't go back to the hospital."

She folded her arms. "I have my reasons. That's all you need to know."

He closed his eyes. *God, why would You do this to me?* But that didn't really matter. He'd dealt with brain tumors before, quite a few of them. Besides, she was not his wife, and just because she was refusing treatment didn't mean that her case was anything like Brigitte's. He really had no choice about what to do with her, though.

"I'll take you somewhere else."

The thought had been hovering in the back of his mind since he'd realized her van was gone, but he knew that it would mean prolonged inter-action with her, and he really didn't want that. Yet, he *was* a doctor. He would do what he had to do to take care of her until she left his realm of influence.

"Where?" she asked, narrowing her eyes at him.

He had to make himself say it. "I know some older ladies who routinely open their home to those in need of a place to stay. It's a large, ante-bellum mansion called Chatam House, so there's plenty of room."

"Antebellum," she echoed. "That means pre–Civil War."

"Yes."

Interest kindled in her mottled-green eyes. "Cool. But what makes you so sure I can crash there?"

"They're very generous. I've never known them to turn away anyone. Besides, they're family friends."

She tilted her head. "You'd do that for me? Ask family friends to take me in?"

"It wouldn't be the first time I've asked the Chatam sisters to take in a pa—er—person."

"No? What other *patients* have you asked these sisters to take in?" she asked, grinning at him.

Brooks looked her straight in the eye. "You know I cannot tell you that." Though the Chatam sisters probably would. One of the patients had married their niece Kaylie. Morgan's wife, Lyla Simone—whom he should have been sitting with at the dinner table just then—had been another.

Eva grinned and swayed toward him, scarves wafting, long pale hair glimmering. Even knowing about her medical and financial troubles, he had to admit that he'd never seen a more exotic, graceful, breathtaking sight. He prayed that she would refuse so he could wash his hands of her.

She did not.

"Okay. I guess I can stand a little antebellum mansion. Just until I can figure out what to do next."

He gulped, disappointed and strangely, horrifyingly pleased. "Let's say at least until your stitches come out, shall we?" he suggested, catching her by the arm as she made to walk past him.

After a moment more of consideration, she agreed. "That ought to do it."

"Do I have your word on that?"

At least she didn't give her word lightly; she actually thought it over before nodding. "You have my word."

"Let's go, then." He walked her to the car, without releasing her arm, and handed her down into it.

"What about my things? My van is stuffed with my things."

"We'll have to get them tomorrow."

She sat back with a huff, her plastic bag in her lap. He closed the door and walked around the rear of the car. On the way, he took out his phone and called Chatam House. He was bringing his best friend's aunties another foundling, and he hoped that she wasn't going to break all their hearts.

Homeless. She had gotten used to the idea of having no permanent address, no brick-and-mortar residence, but Eva couldn't shake the feeling that she had truly hit bottom now that the van was gone. She'd felt strangely *connected* to home, if not particularly comfortable or safe—whatever that meant now—sleeping in the van. One of the reasons she'd decided to hit the road after her diagnosis was the ease with which she could customize the interior of the old minivan. She'd simply pulled out the rear seats and installed a cot, along with her art supplies and the little clothing that she owned. It didn't take much wardrobe to work from home transcribing recorded medical notes, and when money was tight, why bother buying clothes no one would see?

For some reason, her homelessness felt particularly acute when she caught sight of Chatam House. The large, Greek Revival–style, white-painted brick house sat atop a slight rise at the apex of a long, looping drive. With a deep front porch, a fancy kind of carport on its western side, rose arbor and one of the tallest magnolia trees that Eva had ever seen, the place presented a kind of elegance and gentility that belonged to a past era. From the instant the sedan turned through the fat brick columns and drove past the ornate wrought iron gate at the bottom of the hill, Eva felt a sense of peace and serenity, something that had been in short supply in her life even before she'd received her diagnosis. She also felt out of place, disconnected.

"About my things. How can I be sure the bank won't take the van before I can get my clothes and all my other stuff out of there?"

Sighing, Leland brought the car to a halt and pulled out his cell phone to make a phone call. She listened to his end of the conversation with some satisfaction and no little envy.

"Nothing like *cl-out*," she quipped, giving the last word two syllables.

"The van will be there when we go to pick up your things tomorrow," Leland assured her dryly.

"Thank you," she returned crisply, turning her gaze to the side. "And you're sure this is a private home? I mean, how many houses have names?"

He chuckled. "It's a private home, occupied by four older people in their seventies. One of the triplets is married. They have a live-in staff of three as well, but they have quarters out back in the carriage house."

"Triplets?" Eva echoed, laughing.

"Didn't I say? The three sisters are triplets."

"They aren't identical, are they?"

He grinned. "Don't worry. You'll have no problem telling them apart."

The car moved on up the hill and came to a stop in front of a red brick walkway. Leland killed the engine and got out, hurrying around the front of the car. The headlamps had not shut off yet, and Eva was struck again by the strength of the doctor's physical attraction. Instinctively, she understood that he expected to get the door for her, and suddenly she dared not allow it. Yanking on the door handle, she literally bailed out—and nearly planted her face in his collar.

"Hang on," he yelped as she slipped and slid in the deep gravel of the drive.

She found herself seized by the upper arms and

steadied against the solid wall of his chest. The headlamps shut off abruptly, leaving them frozen, nose-to-nose, in the silent dark.

After a moment, his grip loosened, then he calmly asked, "Are you all right?"

"Fine," she muttered. "Stupid shoes." Nodding, he stepped away. "I have some smart ones in the van," she quipped lightly.

He just turned toward the house, one hand fastened to her upper arm as if she couldn't be trusted to find her own way. After escorting her up a trio of steps, he ushered her across the gray-painted floor of the porch to the bright yellow door. A fanlight of bubbly glass over the door offered a cheery glow. Leland knocked, and the door opened only moments later. A balding, roundish, middle-aged fellow wearing black slacks and a white shirt buttoned to the chin smiled in welcome.

"Doctor Brooks."

"Chester. This is Ms. Russell. I believe the aunties are expecting us."

"Yes, sir. I just left the tea tray with them in the front parlor. May I take your coat?"

"Thank you."

"Tea tray?" Eva mused, as Leland divested himself of the overcoat and handed it over.

"Our hostesses enjoy a good cup of tea," he informed her.

She lifted her eyebrows at that, glancing around

the expansive foyer with its golden marble, red mahogany, sweeping staircase and…

"Oh, my. Will you look at that." The ceiling had been painted in sunny shades of blue and yellow and white, a vision of billowing clouds and wafting feathers. "As if ducks have just collided out of sight."

"Ducks colliding?" Leland asked, looking up. "That's what you see?"

"Well, ducks are white," she pointed out lamely. "Some ducks." She had a comical picture of two clumsy ducks crashing together just out of sight and feathers fluttering down.

The doctor shook his head.

Chester cleared his throat. "May I take your, um, wraps, miss?"

"Miss. Oooh. I like it. *Miss* and *young lady* all in one day." She folded her shawls tight. "No, thank you. I think I'll hang on to these. In case I have to make a quick getaway."

Chester's eyebrows leaped all the way up to his nonexistent hairline. Sighing, the doctor clamped a hand around her elbow and tugged her toward a wide doorway.

"We'll show ourselves in, Chester. Give my love to Hilda."

The balding head nodded. Leland towed her into a large room filled with antiques and flowers. Eva glanced around. "Wow. It's like a museum in here."

"I'm afraid that includes the occupants, as well," said an amused, cultured voice.

Eva turned her smile on the speaker, a silver-haired woman peering around the wing of a high-backed, gold-striped chair. The doctor rushed to make the introductions.

"Ladies and gentleman, allow me to present Eva Belle Russell. Eva, Miss Hypatia Kay Chatam."

"Silk and pearls," Eva said, nodding at the dignified lady with the silver chignon and sensible pumps.

"Miss Magnolia Faye Chatam," Leland went on.

"Cardigans and penny loafers," Eva announced, grinning at the wiry woman, her steel gray braid hanging over her shoulder.

"And this is their sister, Odelia May, or more properly, Mrs. Kent Monroe."

Eva laughed aloud, taking in the flamboyant woman's purple turban, fluffy white curls winging out beneath it, the carved parrots swinging from her earlobes and the colorful caftan that clashed so violently with the gold brocade of the love seat where she sat.

"Kindred spirit!" Eva exclaimed, whipping off her shawls and pointing at Odelia, who clapped and stood, holding out both arms to show off the caftan, which had been painted to look like a parrot's chest and wings. "Turn around! Turn around!" Eva urged. Odelia did so, and sure enough, there was the parrot's tail painted onto the silk. "I love it."

Odelia and her husband laughed approvingly. He lumbered to his feet, showing off his pale yellow shirt, turquoise vest and dark purple suit. Beside her Brooks Leland pinched his temples between the thumb and pinky of one hand before saying, "And this, of course, is Mr. Kent Monroe."

"Do me. Describe me," urged Kent. "You're very perspicacious. What do you see?"

Eva swept him with her gaze. Dared she say it? Of course she did. "An Easter egg in a suit."

He and his wife gasped at each other then collapsed with laughter. "Very good! I almost wore a robin's egg blue shirt with this, but as the darling wife pointed out, robins are not parrots."

"And Easter eggs are?" Eva asked, puzzled.

"No, but they're more colorful," the missus said.

"So they are," Eva agreed, winking. "Clever."

"My word, there are two of them now," observed Penny Loafers dryly from the armchair at the end of the low, oblong table before the love seat.

"Would you like a cup of tea, Miss Russell?" asked Silk-and-Pearls.

"Sure, why not?" she replied, taking a seat in one of a pair of armless chairs placed at the opposite end of the tea table from…Magnolia?

Silk-and-Pearls reached for the heavy silver tea-pot. "Brooks, dear?"

"Please," he said, taking the chair beside Eva, "and thank you, Hypatia. I seem to have missed my dinner."

"Hypatia," Eva mused, "wasn't she a Greek mathematician?"

"Why, yes," the current Hypatia said, passing Eva a cup of tea, "as well as a philosopher and astronomer, though very few people seem to know it. How is it that you know about her?"

"Couldn't tell you," Eva admitted. "I remember some things and forget others." She helped herself to several spoonfuls of sugar and looked to the wiry one. "Magnolia is self-explanatory, but I find that names often portend personality and outcomes, so what's your story?"

"Oh, Magnolia grows things," the flamboyant one supplied. "Flowers especially."

"Really?" She waved a spoon at the large, colorful arrangement standing on a small table in the center of the room. "Did you do that?"

Magnolia inclined her head. "I do all the flowers around here."

"Excellent balance and composition. I'm sort of an artist, I know these things."

"Why, thank you."

Eva sipped her tea, made a face and looked to the third sister. "Odelia means wealthy."

"It does," said Odelia, beaming wide enough to set the parrots swinging from her earlobes.

"And are you? Wealthy, I mean."

Odelia glanced around helplessly for a moment, but then she blinked and said, "I think we're all wealthy, really."

Eva wagged a finger. "But you're the real deal, aren't you? You're all quite comfortable, I imagine, but you…" She lifted an eyebrow at Kent. "You married deep pockets there, didn't you? Eh? Mr. Money Bags?"

Hypatia and her sister gaped at the Easter egg, who flushed a deep red, cleared his throat and said, "I've made no secret of the fact that I've done quite well. I paid for the wedding, the remodeling of the upstairs, the pool…" He patted Odelia's hand, where an enormous diamond rested. "Whatever my darling desires."

Odelia giggled like a girl.

"Awww," Eva crooned, "that's so sweet. At your ages people are usually sick of the sight of each other."

Beside her, Dr. Leland choked on a swallow of his own tea. "Tell them," he croaked.

"What?"

"Tell them or I will."

"I don't know what you're talking about."

"Eva has a medical condition," Leland said, "and if she's going to stay here you need to know about it."

Hypatia handed cups to her sisters. "We assumed that was the case."

"Duh," muttered Eva. "The doctor calls—someone's sick." Brooks sent her a stern, almost sullen glare. "Just saying."

"One of the symptoms of her condition seems to be a lack of an internal monitor."

"That's a nasty thing to say!" Eva squawked. "It's not like I blurt inappropriate words or things that don't make sense. I'm just honest. What's wrong with that?"

"Not all honesty is socially acceptable," he snapped. "If you were thinking normally, you would recognize that fact."

"I'm perfectly normal," she shot back, "except for the brain tumor!"

Three cups hit three saucers. She heard a gasp and a tiny moan. Looking around, she saw that the Chatam sisters were all staring at the doctor with looks of utter dismay.

"Oh, Brooks," Hypatia said.

He shook his head. "It's not like Brigitte's situation."

Brigitte? Eva glanced around. Who was Brigitte?

"I deal with things like this all the time," he went on. "You're not to worry about me."

Him? They were worried about *him*?

"What is it with you?" Eva asked, slumping. "I'm the one with the brain tumor, and they're all worried about *you*? What's a girl got to do to catch a break around you?"

"You don't understand," Brooks began.

At the same time, Hypatia said, "Oh, my dear, we're concerned for you, of course. We'll be praying for you diligently."

"Swell," Eva drawled.

Odelia sighed, a hand going to her cheek. "You're not a believer?"

"No way. I've had that church stuff thrown at me my whole life, and what good has it ever done? None."

The doctor bowed his head, murmuring, "Ladies, I'm so sorry. Our acquaintance has been short. She's my patient. I never dreamed she'd be so difficult. I just didn't know what else to do with her."

They all started talking at once.

"No, no."

"It's all right."

"You always do what's best, dear boy."

"It'll be fine. You'll see. God has a purpose."

"It's just that she hit her head while I was in the grocery store and while I was stitching her up her van was repossessed, and she's so broke that she hasn't even been eating." He shook his head. "She won't stay in the hospital. She wouldn't even tell me her name. I had to find out from the police."

"Are you done?" Eva demanded indignantly.

"I am," Leland retorted, shooting to his feet. "I

absolutely am." Bending, he placed his teacup and saucer on the large ornate silver tray and straightened. "Hypatia, Magnolia, Odelia, Kent, my apologies, but I'm leaving now."

Hypatia came to her feet. She might have reached Eva's shoulder, but her dignity stood very tall indeed, regally so. "I'll walk you out."

Odelia and Kent looked at each other and hauled themselves up.

"We'll just make sure Hilda is aware we'll be adding another place for meals," Kent said.

"The, um, bed-sit should be ready," Odelia said to her sister.

Magnolia smiled a slow, challenging smile. "I'll show up our guest."

The Monroes beat a hasty, if colorful, retreat.

Eva smiled at her remaining hostess, quipping, "I wasn't entirely sure I'd be staying."

Magnolia rose, still smiling, and said, "Oh, you're perfectly welcome. Unless you hurt our beloved Brooks. If that happens, I'll put you out myself." With that, she turned and walked across the room.

After a moment, Eva rose and followed.

Chapter Three

"I won't even ask," Morgan said, handing Brooks a steaming mug of something hot, "because you wouldn't tell me anyway."

"Medical emergencies," Brooks murmured, sniffing the mug suspiciously, "cannot be discussed."

"My point exactly," said Morgan, saluting Brooks with his own drink before sipping delicately.

"What is it this time?" Morgan asked, unable to identify the dark liquid in his mug.

"Cranberry punch. I like it."

"You liked the birch bark tea."

Morgan liked anything his lovely, feverishly domestic wife invented.

"Bri loves the stuff," Morgan said in his own defense.

Morgan's thirteen-month-old daughter Brigitte, named for Brooks's late wife, had a cast-iron stomach, a hearty constitution and a wonderfully cheerful disposition. Brooks adored her, and would have even if Morgan and Lyla hadn't named her after his Brigitte. He sipped the cranberry punch and found it palatable.

Bri came into the wood-paneled room perched on her mother's slim hip. After her cancer, Lyla Simone had barely had enough hair to cover her head, but now her light reddish brown hair had grown to chin length, sleekly framing her oval face with its big, gray eyes. Nearly two decades his wife's senior, Morgan's nut-brown hair showed specks of silver, and he had the distinctive cinnamon brown Chatam eyes, as well as the Chatam cleft chin. Bri's thin, pale blond hair and bright blue eyes contrasted with the coloring of both of her parents, but then Bri was adopted, the biological child of a teenager whom Lyla had rescued from an abusive relationship.

The thought struck Brooks that Bri looked more like Eva Belle Russell than Morgan and Lyla. Just the thought of his difficult patient irritated him.

"I'm sorry I missed dinner," he told Lyla, pushing away thoughts of Eva.

Chuckling, Lyla bent and placed a plate on the coffee table between the comfy leather sofa where he sat and the overstuffed armchair where her husband lounged. "No worries. Bri and I went ahead and ate. Now you and Morgan can enjoy yourselves." She handed Bri to her father, and left the library.

"God bless that woman," Brooks said with heartfelt gratitude, helping himself to a thick ham and cheese sandwich.

"Your mommy is a wonder," Morgan told his daughter in a silly voice. "Uncle Brooks is a jealous man."

"Green with envy," Brooks admitted, biting into the sandwich. The time had been when it was the other way around, but Brooks was happy to see his friend happy now, and he loved Lyla and Bri for being the agents of that happiness. He prayed that Morgan's happiness would last many, many years longer than his own had.

Lyla returned to take up her daughter again and cart her off to bed. Bri roused but didn't protest, a child so well loved that she felt no reason to fear. This, too, made Brooks smile. As soon as mother and daughter left the room, however, he frowned, knowing that he had to speak of a subject he'd rather not broach.

"I have imposed upon your aunts again."

Morgan sat up straight in his chair and leaned forward. "Oh? How so? Another celebrity patient?"

The last "celebrity patient" had been the goalie for a professional Fort Worth hockey team injured in an accident and needing to recuperate away from the limelight. He was now Morgan's brother-in-law.

"Just the opposite, I'm afraid," Brooks admitted. "This one is something of an itinerant, too broke to eat, let alone provide shelter for herself until she's healed, so…"

"So it's the aunties to the rescue once again."

"What would we do without them?" Brooks asked.

"I shudder to think."

"Just thought I should let you know," Brooks said, realizing the time had come to go. Lyla would be waiting for her husband to join her.

He got up from the sofa and reached for his overcoat. Morgan didn't try to stop him. He rose, too, and walked around the coffee table, sliding his hands into the pockets of his slacks.

"What's her name?" he asked. "This itinerant patient of yours."

"Eva Belle Russell."

They walked together out of the library and across the terra cotta tile floor of the expansive living room of Morgan's graceful 1928 house.

"Older lady?" he mused. "Eva Belle."

"Not particularly," Brooks hedged.

"No? How old is she then?" Morgan wanted to know.

Brooks shrugged into his coat. "Oh, mid-thirties."

"Really?" Morgan tilted his head. "What does she look like?"

Brooks fiddled with his collar. "Tall, thin."

They reached the small foyer and went down the two steps to the arched front door.

"Blonde, brunette, redhead?" Morgan ventured dryly.

Brooks sighed. "She has blond hair."

"Long? Short?"

"Long."

"Blue eyes?"

He considered pretending that he hadn't noticed, but a doctor would have looked into his patient's eyes. Instead, he chose a nonchalant tone. "Green hazelish."

"Pretty, is she?" Morgan pressed, rocking back on his heels.

Brooks tamped down his irritation. Any attempt at prevarication would catch up with Brooks in short order. Might as well face the facts head on. "Stunning, if you must know."

Morgan grinned. It was funny how a little domestic bliss made matchmakers of even the most stalwart former bachelors. Brooks shook his head grimly.

"Don't get any ideas. She's the very last woman on the face of the earth I'd get involved with."

"And why is that?"

Brooks looked his friend in the eye and tossed aside his medical ethics. "She has a brain tumor."

The nascent spark of hope there swiftly died. "Oh, hey, I'm sorry."

"She's not Brigitte," Brooks said softly. "It's not like that. Well, Eva *is* refusing treatment for some reason, but it's not my problem, and it's not going to be."

"No, of course, it isn't," Morgan rushed to say. "No one would expect—"

"She's just passing through," Brooks broke in. "She's not my problem."

"That's right," Morgan agreed, frowning uncertainly.

Brooks nodded. "Well, I have a busy day tomorrow. Give Lyla my thanks, and kiss Bri good-night for me."

"Sure," Morgan said, opening the door, "but, Brooks…"

"Yeah?"

"You could kiss Bri good-night yourself."

He could, but he wouldn't. That was a dad's job. Brooks clapped his friend on the upper arm as he slid through the door. "Sleep well."

"You, too."

Brooks flashed Morgan a wave as he hurried to his waiting car. He thought of the cold, dark house waiting for him, and as he drove away from Morgan's warm, comfortable home, he tried not to feel sorry for himself. He'd had his time in the sun. He'd won the girl and made the most of what they'd been given. He had no regrets on that score. But now, sixteen years later, he could be forgiven for a touch of melancholy, couldn't he?

It would pass. Somehow, he couldn't help thinking that it would pass just as soon as Eva Russell left town. Somehow he knew he'd feel better again once she had gone on her way. Then things could get back to normal.

Why normal had recently begun to feel less than satisfactory, he did not know or want to.

The room, if it could be called that, was downright luxurious, from the thick, cream-colored carpet underfoot to the royal blue velvet sofa and chairs in the sitting area and the cream-painted wood paneling. The bed furniture looked to be Empire-style, unless Eva missed her guess. Whatever the period, it was the real deal—no reproductions here. Sky-blue velvet curtains trimmed in heavy gold cording and fringe adorned the windows, with white on cream in the bathroom, gold fittings and sea-green towels. Vases of vibrant coral roses shocked the senses and perfumed the air, their color picked up in the subtle paintings on the walls. Over the stately fireplace hung a thoroughly modern flat-screen television.

Magnolia Chatam invited Eva to run a hot bath in the jetted tub and went out to find an extra nightgown for her. Deciding to take her up on the offer, Eva gingerly pulled up her hair and piled it atop her head. The blood had been rinsed out of it when the wound had been cleansed, but it could use a good scrubbing. That, however, would have to wait until her stitches came out. She began to disrobe, removing her scarves one by one and folding them carefully. Who knew how long she would have to wear the things?

She was down to her leggings and turtleneck when Magnolia returned with a voluminous cotton gown and a flannel robe that might have been fashionable in the 1920s.

"So you've always tried to look hideous," Eva surmised, realizing she'd spoken aloud only when she heard the other woman's gasp. "Oh, I said that, didn't I? Maybe I do need the speech police." She folded the flannel robe against her and made a face. "Sorry."

Magnolia rolled her eyes, but then a reluctant smile tugged at her pursed lips. "Convenient thing, this brain tumor of yours. I've often wished for an unassailable reason to speak my mind."

"Always has to be an up side," Eva said. "That's what I told my ex when I caught him in bed with another woman."

Magnolia drew back, obviously horrified. "Oh, my. What possible 'up side' could there be to that?"

Eva almost said, "No custody battle." Instead she quipped, "The prenup was nullified, for one thing."

Magnolia blinked. "Well, I guess that was something."

"Would've been if he hadn't blown everything

on bad investments," Eva told her offhandedly. "Anyway, thanks for the nightclothes. Doc says we'll get my own things from the van tomorrow."

"The, ah, robe was my father's," Magnolia confessed.

"Yeah?" Eva held up the striped flannel garment and really looked at it.

"I often wear his things," Magnola said, lifting her chin. "I hate waste, and they suit me far better than silks and bows."

Eva smiled at the older woman. "Okay. I can get with that." She glanced at the nightgown and said, "I don't suppose you have any of his pajamas, do you?"

Magnolia chuckled. "I'll fetch you a pair."

"You're a peach," Eva told her. "Just leave them on the bed. I'm getting in that tub."

"Fine," Magnolia agreed. "I've had the kitchen send up a tray for you. You'll find it in the dumbwaiter out on the landing when you're ready for it."

"You're kidding," Eva gushed. "That's super! Thanks." She wrinkled her nose and asked, "Tea?"

"Apple cider," Magnolia assured her.

Eva threw back her head in grateful glee, then grabbed it as a sharp pain burned her scalp. "That's wonderful. I've died and gone to heaven."

Her hostess stilled, hands folded. "That, my dear, is something we need to discuss."

Eva heaved out a deep breath. "Look," she said,

letting her hands fall to her sides, "I've heard it all before. Christ on the cross. God is love, answering our prayers, if we're good little girls. It's all malarkey."

Magnolia shook her wizened head. "Oh, child, what has happened to make you think such things?"

"Hmm, let's see." Eva ticked off the issues on her fingers. "A father I never knew. A mother and a sister who both died of cancer. A lying cheat of a husband. Oh, and a tumor in my head slowly killing me. Let's see, did I forget the aunt who took a strap to my backside every time I turned around then gave our food money to the church? Yeah, give me some more of that."

Magnolia looked positively stricken. For a moment, Eva thought the old woman might cry, but then she blinked, stiffened her already straight spine and said, "I blame your mother for your brain tumor."

Eva literally reeled backward. "What?"

"I blame her for your terrible taste in men."

Gaping, Eva sputtered, "H-how dare you!"

"I could even blame her for your sister's cancer. It's often hereditary, after all."

Blazingly angry, Eva fisted her hands, a vein throbbing painfully in her head. "That's not fair! You take that back!"

"But you blame God for the failures of His children and the problems of a fallen world," Magnolia pointed out, shrugging.

Eva's eyes narrowed, and some of her anger waned as she caught on to Magnolia's game. "That's different," Eva grated out. "My mother was human. God is all-powerful."

"Is He?" Magnolia returned. "All-powerful but stupid, I take it."

"Of course not. I never said that. Don't put words in my mouth."

"Then, cruel."

"Yes!" she crowed triumphantly. "Absolutely."

"Cruel enough to let Himself be crucified to pay the sin debt for the whole of humanity," Magnolia said. "Cruel enough to give that same humanity the free will to reject His sacrifice." She clucked her tongue. "You have a funny definition of cruel, Ms. Russell. I suspect your definition of cruel is simply not getting what you want when and how you want it."

Eva was still grasping for a reply when the door closed behind her hostess. She was still standing there several moments later, clutching that old flannel robe, when the thought occurred that Magnolia Chatam didn't need the excuse of a brain tumor to speak her mind, and as hard as she tried to be angry about that, Eva couldn't help admiring the old girl.

She made sure that she was in the tub when Magnolia returned with the pajamas, and she stayed there until her skin puckered and pruned. Then, dressed in the Chatam sisters' father's nightclothes, she stuck her head out of the door to her room and made sure that the landing was deserted before she padded on bare feet to the dumbwaiter and fetched the tray laden with a steaming pot of apple cider, the most scrumptious muffins imaginable and a selection of cheeses and fruit.

Pigging out, she ate as much as she possibly could. After all, she assumed that there would be more where this came from, but after she left here, who knew when she'd eat again? She lay back on the bed, utterly replete, and contemplated her next move.

The medication she'd received earlier had relieved the pressure inside her skull and probably bought her some time. Otherwise, her language would still be messed up. It had frightened her to hear herself speaking gibberish again. She'd known it was a possibility, of course, but because she'd been getting dizzy and even blacking out, she'd assumed that she'd simply continue on that path until she just wouldn't wake up one day. She supposed she'd have to find a way to fill her prescriptions again, at least until she found a permanent place to crash, but she could make that decision later. First she had to think about transportation—and decide whether or not to call Ricky.

She'd promised herself that she wouldn't, not

until she'd found a permanent place to let it end, but without the van, that place might be closer than she'd anticipated. She checked the time, saw that it was fairly late, and told herself to let it go another day, but somehow she found herself with her phone in hand, her thumbs punching in the familiar numbers.

Ricky himself answered on the second ring. "Allenson residence."

He wouldn't know it was her because she'd blocked the number, but she imagined that she heard a hopeful tone in his voice.

"Hey, Ricky. How's it going, big guy?"

"Mom! I knew it was you. I knew it."

She tried not to choke up. "You sound good. How's it going, hon?"

"When are you coming home?" he demanded, ignoring her question. "I hate it here. I want to go home."

His complaints hit her like blows to her chest. She closed her eyes and fought to keep her tone light. "Ricky, your dad would be crushed to hear you say that."

"I don't care. I hate Tiffany. She treats me like a five-year-old."

"That's because she's a mental five-year-old," Eva muttered. Louder she said, "Give her a break, Ricky. She's never been a mom, and she's still learning."

"You say that like she *can* learn. Mom, I want to go with you."

Eva's throat clogged, but she cleared it and said, "Son, you're better off with your father now."

"He's never here! Neither of them are."

Eva sat up. "They're leaving you unsupervised?"

"No," he admitted reluctantly. "Donita's here."

Breathing a sigh of relief, Eva slumped back onto the bed. Donita was the housekeeper that she and Rick, her ex, had employed before their marriage had ended so ingloriously. If Donita was there then Rick must have recouped some of his financial losses.

"That's good," Eva said. "That's very good." Donita was trustworthy and loyal. She would look after Ricky. She had kept in touch when Eva had struggled to keep a roof over their heads and study, too. "You do what Donita tells you," Eva instructed, "and tell her that I said 'Thanks.' Will you do that?"

"I wish you'd just come home," he whined.

"I know," Eva told him. "I would if I could, son."

"But why can't you?" he asked.

"I just can't. It's best for you that I don't."

"Adults always say that when they just don't want to explain," he complained.

She chuckled, trying to sound carefree. "You think so, do you? Well, you'll figure it out one of these days. You just remember that everything I do, I do to spare you misery. Okay?"

"Making me live with Tiffany isn't sparing me misery," he told her grumpily.

She laughed. It was either that or sob. "I love you."

"Yeah, yeah," he groused, but then he muttered, "I love you, too."

She could barely speak again after that. Managing to squeak out a "Good night," she broke the connection, clutched the phone to her chest and wept until sleep at last overcame her.

"Poor girl," Odelia opined, tears glistening in her eyes. She glanced longingly at the door that connected the sisters' sitting room to the suite she shared with Kent. Strangely, marriage had somehow enlarged Odelia. She was no less scatterbrained or flamboyant—indeed, she seemed rather more so, as Kent encouraged her shamelessly—yet, she had somehow grown more confident and *knowing*.

"Poor Brooks," Hypatia said. "The last thing he needs, with Morgan now happily married, is a reminder of all he has lost."

"This is true," Magnolia admitted, "and yet, if we've learned anything over the years, we've learned that God has plans and reasons for what and whom He brings into this house."

Her sisters murmured their agreement, nodding.

"Our first concern," Magnolia went on, "must be Eva herself. Perhaps my fear that she is dying is unfounded, but her spiritual condition is not. She blatantly admitted her lack of faith."

"Brooks originally stated that she would be staying only until her stitches could be removed," Hypatia revealed, "so our time with her is limited, regardless of the true state of her health."

"Then, there's no time to lose," Magnolia decided. "She won't like it, but we need to get her to prayer meeting tomorrow night."

"And how do you suggest we do that?" Hypatia asked, sounding tired. She tugged the collar of her navy blue silk robe closer about her throat. Magnolia noted idly that its white piping looked very like her skin, which seemed unusually pale tonight.

"Leave Eva to me," Magnolia said, waving a hand. "Are you cold, sister?"

"This winter has seemed interminable," Hypatia complained. "I'm off to my warm bed." She heaved herself out of the armchair where she customarily sat for these late evening chats. The sisters routinely spoke and prayed together at the end of the day, and Magnolia was glad that hadn't changed with Odelia's marriage a couple years ago.

"Good night, dear," Odelia said, uncurling from the corner of the sofa.

"Good night."

"Kent thinks she needs a good multivitamin," Odelia whispered as soon as the door closed behind their sister's back.

Magnolia blinked. She hadn't noticed that Hypatia needed anything, though perhaps she had seemed to suffer more from the cold this winter than in years past. Kent, being a pharmacist, would know about these things, though.

"Getting her the vitamins and getting her to take them are two different things," Magnolia murmured. "Maybe we should speak to Brooks about it."

"Hmm," Odelia considered. "Perhaps so, though perhaps not just now."

Magnolia smiled. "I suspect the right time will come."

"It always does," Odelia said with a giggle, hurrying toward her private suite and her waiting husband.

Magnolia sighed and shook her head. It had come for Odelia after fifty years, and the result seemed to be one long honeymoon. She prayed that Eva Russell's time for joy would come before it was too late. Hers and dear Brooks's.

Chapter Four

She woke hungry. Nothing new in that. Eva rolled over, opening her eyes, and everything abruptly changed. The bed beneath her did not squeak and groan or smell of plastic. She was not locked, crammed, into the back of her funky old van. Instead, light and opulence flooded her senses. Memory rushed over her, beginning with the scrumptious doctor who had tended her the day before and ending with the wizened old gardening gnome who had delivered the pajamas that Eva currently wore. She thought of Magnolia pugnaciously standing up to her last night.

I blame your mother for your brain tumor. I blame her for your terrible taste in men. I could even blame her for your sister's cancer. It's often hereditary, after all...You blame God for the failures of His children and the problems of a fallen world...let Himself be crucified to pay the sin debt for the whole of humanity...and give that same humanity the free will to reject His sacrifice. I suspect your definition of cruel is simply not getting what you want when and how you want it.

Eva had to admit that she had a point. If people possessed free will, it didn't seem quite fair to blame God for everything they did. And while Eva wasn't completely sure what the "problems of a fallen world" meant, she'd never before thought of the crucifixion as payment for sin debt. She tried to square that with some of the things she'd heard her aunt say, but her stomach rumbled, so she quickly moved on. Throwing back the covers, she sat up and looked around her.

The stitches pulled on the back of her head and pain knocked on her skull, but the room didn't tilt, so she threw her legs over the side of the bed and put her feet on the floor. After quickly dressing, she used a new toothbrush that she found in a drawer in the bathroom, then went out in search of a meal, leaving all but a single shawl behind. She met Magnolia, also dressed much as she had been the night before, on the landing at the head of the stairs.

"Good morning. Sleep well?"

"I did," Eva answered, tying the shawl about her waist. "How about you, Penny Loafers?"

Magnolia lifted her eyebrows but answered sedately. "Always. Ready for breakfast?"

"Does a bear, uh, live in the woods?" And the doc said she had no internal monitor.

Magnolia blinked at her. "I would imagine so, yes."

"Well, there you go, then."

Blink, blink. "Ah. Hm. Let's go down, then. I'll show you the way to the sunroom where we breakfast."

As they descended the broad staircase, which turned back on itself halfway down, Eva gazed upward at the ceiling. On second perusal, it did seem too ethereal for comic ducks.

"Maybe doves," she murmured.

"I beg your pardon?"

"The ceiling." She pointed upward. "Who painted it?"

"No one knows," Magnolia told her. "The records were long since lost. It is a work of art, though. Wouldn't you agree?"

"Oh, yeah. It's something, all right," Eva muttered.

Still craning her neck to take it all in, she almost missed the bottom step and nearly pitched onto her face. Only Magnolia's cry and Eva's grasp on the curled banister saved her. Stumbling into the bottom post, Eva righted herself in the nick of time.

"Whoa!" she joked, swiping at her scarf. "Remind me not to go walking around looking up while my stomach's empty and I have stitches in the back of my head."

Magnolia set her pruned mouth and grasped Eva by the wrist, instructing, "This way."

The old girl proved surprisingly strong as she towed Eva down one of a pair of hallways flanking the grand staircase to the sunroom at the very end. A colorful combination of rattan furnishings, tropical prints, potted plants, a rock fireplace and glass walls overlooking an enormous patio and a large, covered pool, the long, narrow room managed to feel sunny and warm despite the gray, cold day. Most compelling of all, however, was the table laden with pots of tea and, thankfully, coffee, crisp bacon, scrambled eggs, fresh fruit and steaming oatmeal.

"I'm going to kiss the cook," Eva exclaimed, pulling out a chair, "right after I pig out."

Magnolia chuckled, seating herself. "What will you have?"

"Just don't let any body parts get too close to my plate."

Clucking her tongue to hide her smile, Magnolia poured tea for herself while Eva heaped her plate. A large woman with brownish-gray, chin-length hair came out of a side door and carried a basket of ridiculously fragrant muffins to the table.

"Hilda," Magnolia said, "this is our guest, Miss Eva Belle Russell. Miss Russell—"

Shielding her full mouth behind her hand, Eva corrected her. "Eva. Just Eva."

"Eva," Magnolia went on, "this is our cook, Mrs. Hilda Worth. Her husband, Chester—"

Whatever else she might have said got lost when Eva jumped up and smacked a kiss on Hilda's cheek.

Hilda screeched an "Oh!" and started to laugh. "That hungry, are you? I was told to fatten you up. No one said you were starving."

"I'll kiss your feet to keep eating like this," Eva said, dropping back into her chair and reaching for a muffin. She brought it to her nose and inhaled deeply. Lately she'd found that she couldn't always smell as well as she should, but the ginger aroma made her head swim. Biting off a huge chunk, she let the flavors infuse her mouth before she chewed, moaning with delight, and swallowed. Hilda waddled back into the kitchen, chuckling and shaking her head.

"You've made a friend there," Magnolia told her. "Feel free to help yourself to anything in the kitchen that doesn't need cooking, and if you like reading or want to use the computer, I'll show you the library."

That caused Eva to pause in her feeding. "You have a real library?"

Magnolia nodded. "And a music room. Just off the ballroom."

"You're pulling my leg."

"Hardly."

"Huh. Sure beats a roadside park for amenities."

Eva went on eating, aware that she was behaving like a perfect glutton but unable to help herself. It had been so long since she had been able to simply eat her fill that she couldn't stop until she was stuffed. When she finally put down her fork, Magnolia was looking a little worried.

"Are you going to keep all that down?"

"I think so, but if you don't mind, I'm just going to sit here for a minute to let it all settle. I wouldn't want to upset the Muffin Queen by upchucking her delicious food."

Magnolia laughed, waved a knobby hand and picked up her teacup, long since having finished her own breakfast. Eva stretched out her legs beneath the table and folded her hands over her packed middle.

"The doc said he'd take me to get my things out of my van today."

"It's his half day at the office," Magnolia told her, "so I imagine he'll be around this afternoon, but I can call him to remind him, just in case."

"Ah. You know him pretty well, then."

"I should say so. We've known Brooks Harris Leland his entire life."

Eva sat up straight again. "Do tell."

Magnolia looked down, picking up stray crumbs from the tabletop with her fingertip and transferring them to her plate. "He's a family friend, the best friend of our nephew Morgan. His father was paralyzed in a fall when Brooks was in grade school and died while he was in college. His mother wore herself out taking care of her husband and died before Brooks married."

"He's a widower, right? He mentioned his late wife last night."

Magnolia's amber gaze speared Eva's. "That's right. His wife, Brigitte, died only a few years after they married."

"And he hasn't remarried?"

"No. It's been, oh, sixteen, seventeen years, and he's never remarried, never even come close, that I know of."

Eva realized that her mouth hung open and snapped it shut. "Dr. Gorgeous has been single for *that* long?"

Lifting her eyebrows, Magnolia disciplined a smile. "He is rather…handsome, isn't he?"

Rolling her eyes, Eva said, "Yeah, well, there's eye candy and there's *handsome*. In my book, handsome is as handsome does."

"And as I said, Brooks is handsome," Magnolia insisted. "He's a fine Christian man."

"Which is three reasons to avoid him," Eva told herself, only to realize that she'd spoken aloud when Magnolia frowned at her.

"Three reasons?"

Eva cleared her throat. So much for that interior monitor. Still, might as well lay it out for the old girl. "One, he's a doctor."

"Not usually a negative," Magnolia mused, obviously confused.

"Two, he's gorgeous."

"Again, not usually a strike against a man."

"And three," Eva went on, only to realize that number three might actually insult her hostess, an outspoken Christian. "He, um, is obviously still in love with his late wife."

"I suppose that might be true," Magnolia mused, frowning.

"How about kids?" Eva asked, more to distract Magnolia than from any true desire for an answer. As a rule, she tried not to think about other people and their kids.

"None, sadly," Magnolia told her with a shake of her iron-gray head.

"Well, at least he's not raising them alone," Eva said, quickly adding, "I mean, since he hasn't remarried. I can see why he might not, really. If his experience with happily-ever-after was anything like mine, he'll have sworn off forever-after, believe me."

"You've been very hurt, haven't you?" Magnolia observed more than asked. "Was your husband a professing Christian then?"

Eva snorted. "Not hardly."

"Perhaps that was part of the problem," Magnolia suggested before abruptly getting to her feet. "Now, let me show you the library."

Sheepishly, Eva got up and let the garden gnome

in her cardigan and penny loafers lead her back through the house to the library just off the foyer across from the formal parlor.

First a phone call, and then an ambush. Brooks tamped down his irritation and smiled at Magnolia, who looked like a shrunken version of her late father, albeit with a braid gracing one shoulder. The fact that she wore a pair of Hubner's old galoshes and huddled inside his old overcoat added to the illusion. She might even be wearing his old eyeglasses at the moment. Doubtless, she was also encased in one of Hub Sr.'s old cardigan sweaters under that voluminous coat. Magnolia did not wait there on the porch of Chatam House in the cold January sunshine so he could admire her frugal, androgynous style, however. Like her phone call reminding him that he had promised to take Eva to retrieve her personal belongings from her impounded van, this did not bode well for his peace of mind. Inwardly he sighed.

"What has she done?"

Magnolia waved a gnarled hand. "So far as I know Eva hasn't done anything but eat and read. I am deeply concerned with her spiritual condition, though, especially as I suspect she is *very* unwell."

Magnolia stood no taller than his shoulder, but when she looked up at him with those stern, steady amber eyes of hers, she—more so than her sisters—made him feel all of ten years old again. He resisted the urge to clear his throat and shuffle his feet.

"You already know that she has a brain tumor. Beyond that, I cannot tell you a thing."

"Such frightening words, *brain tumor*," Magnolia mused, turning away, "but I don't have to tell you that."

"No."

"Still, great strides have been made in treatment."

"Indeed."

"Many new treatments are now available."

"True."

"I understand that some tumors are now treated with drugs alone." She looked over her shoulder then, pinning him with a gaze so direct that he knew he was being probed. He was almost glad that he didn't have answers to give her, answers he could not have given her, anyway, for ethical reasons.

"Some," he returned succinctly.

As if admitting defeat or drawing an unhappy conclusion, she nodded. "And God is still in the healing business."

"He is."

She turned to face him again, her chin aloft. "We've come to the conclusion that we need to get her to prayer meeting." The *we* being Magnolia and her sisters, of course, for whom he would do just about anything, as they well knew.

"Tonight, you mean."

"The sooner the better, wouldn't you say? All things considered."

Well, she had him there. Given Eva's condition and the fact that she would be staying only long enough to let her scalp wound heal, it didn't make any sense to delay.

"I assume you want me to convince her to attend the meeting."

Magnolia's mouth twitched. "I think that in this instance Dr. Gorgeous might have more influence than Penny Loafers, Silk-and-Pearls and Kindred Spirit, not to mention Easter Egg."

Brooks rolled his eyes. "Oh, brother."

"Although Hilda the Muffin Queen runs you a close second at this point," Magnolia informed him from behind her hand.

He laughed. "So her cognitive abilities are not seriously impaired, then."

"Or at least she knows which side of her bread is buttered. Literally," Magnolia teased.

Brooks reached out an arm to escort her into the house, saying playfully, "I think Eva is rubbing off on you."

"She does have a winsome way about her," Magnolia admitted.

"That's one way of putting it," Brooks muttered, letting them into the warmth.

"I believe you'll find her in the library," Magnolia told him.

Brooks unbuttoned his overcoat and walked across the foyer to the open door of the library antechamber. A large red mahogany conference table surrounded by chairs took up most of the space. Beyond that was a small office with a double desk topped by a computer and a broad, lovely space furnished floor-to-ceiling with shelves filled with books. A trio of comfortable chairs flanked by lamps had been arranged around a long low table suitable for a tea tray, of course. Brooks walked past the conference table and the door to the office, turning into the library proper.

He did not at first see anyone. Then a slender foot clad in a black stocking kicked into the air, prompting him to look past the tea table.

"Eva?"

The foot went down, and her head popped up, a smile breaking across her face.

"Doc!" She reared up onto her knees, obviously having been reclining on her stomach on the floor. "You remembered." Beaming, she clutched a book against her chest.

In truth, she had not been far from his thoughts all morning. Then again, he found himself all but unable to speak as she laid the book on the table and got to her feet. She stood before him covered chin to toes in black spandex, a single large colorful scarf tied about her slender waist above one hip, and yet her garb left absolutely nothing to the imagination where her shape was concerned. And how shapely she was!

Given her height, he'd expected her to be all long limbs, but not even his fairly thorough physical examination the day before—which had revealed jutting, if narrow, hip bones, the ridges of her ribs and certain obvious scars—had prepared him for the neat lushness of her curves. Now, without all the fluttering scarves, he saw just how utterly feminine she was, especially given all that sleek, butter-yellow hair falling from a natural center part and the sheer perfection of her long, oval face. If her big cat's eyes had been a more pure green, she'd have brought him to his knees. As it was, he found himself compelled to study their mottled green-gold-and-blue hazel depths.

Thank God she wouldn't be staying long.

He managed some motion with his hands and croaked, "Get your shoes."

She made a hopping motion and kicked up a foot, showing him that she'd stepped into her black, backless mules. "Ta-da!"

He couldn't help smiling. "Okay. Get your coat, then."

"Shawls," she said, all but running for the door. "Give me one minute. Two," she amended, rushing past him. "It's a long staircase."

He shook his head and bent forward to catch the title of the book she'd been reading before following her out into the foyer. It was a book of fairytales. That seemed somehow fitting and, at the same time, sad. She was halfway up the stairs by the time he brushed back his coat and leaned a forearm on the newel post at the bottom. Only when she turned the corner did he realize that he'd been staring at the sway of her neat backside. He spun away, only to find Odelia and Kent staring at him, their heads cocked like a pair of quizzical bluebirds, which seemed to be the day's theme.

Bluebirds bobbed on tiny springs from Odelia's earlobes, complimenting her blue pantsuit, and she wore a blue-feathered headband among her frothy white curls. Kent, meanwhile, wore a robin's egg blue shirt beneath a royal blue suit and blue-on-blue striped bowtie.

"The bluebirds of happiness have arrived," Brooks quipped. Magnolia wasn't the only one Eva seemed to be influencing with her silly wit.

Odelia giggled, and that made Kent preen before he sobered and asked, "Are you quite well, dear boy?"

"Just fine. I'm here to take Eva to retrieve her personal belongings."

"Oh, yesss," Odelia hissed softly. "Poor girl."

Thinking it safer not to be drawn into another conversation concerning her health, Brooks merely nodded, but Odelia had other concerns.

"What will she do now, do you think?"

"Um, well, she'll stay here until her stitches are removed, and then...I assume she'll move along."

"How will she do that without transportation?" Kent asked.

Brooks had avoided thinking about that very thing. "I imagine she has a plan."

"She doesn't strike me as the planning sort," Odelia confided softly. "She seems more a wanderer, flitting about from pillar to post, but without her vehicle, how will she get there?"

"I don't know," Brooks admitted, "but she seems pretty resourceful to me."

Eva came tripping down the stairs just then, literally. She all but fell onto the foyer floor, clattered to a stop and whipped her layers of fringed shawls around her shoulders. "Ready!"

"Where's your coat?" Odelia asked.

Eva tossed the corner of a silky shawl over one shoulder. "This is my coat."

Dismayed, Odelia brought her hands up to cover her mouth, which had formed a perfect O.

Patting a bluebird so that it bounced on the end of its spring, Eva quipped, "Be happy, little bluebird. The doc won't let the elements get me. Not yet, anyway." She winked at Odelia then and clomped to the door in her fluttery, multicolored costume.

Brooks tried to give Odelia a reassuring smile and strode after Eva. *Not yet, anyway.* What was that supposed to mean? For some reason, he remembered that book of fairytales on the table back there in the library. What a dichotomy this woman was, one that he truly did not want to investigate. Now, if only he knew why God had brought her into his life at this particular moment, perhaps he could get her out of it again and put away thoughts of her once and for all.

"Thank you for stopping for the boxes," she said, lifting the seat on the wood trunk she'd had bolted to the floorboard behind the driver's seat of her van.

"No problem," Brooks said, watching through the open tailgate of the van. He'd parked his car in the traffic lane behind the van and opened the trunk, as instructed by the attendant of the impound yard. Now he waited for her to hand him what needed to be transferred from her vehicle to his.

She lifted a stack of clothing from the trunk: two pairs of jeans, half a dozen T-shirts, a short cardigan, a long, slim knit skirt, all in solid colors. These she placed in one box. On top of them she placed a black beret, a pink baseball cap with a bejeweled brim and a handful of bandanas. In another box she stashed her favorite red high heels and a pair of turquoise cowboy boots, along with a pair of belts and a tan pocketbook, as well as her toiletries. The third box contained her art supplies, including the mini microwave oven that she used to cure some projects. She chewed her bottom lip over the few dishes, butane stove and folding cot that comprised the remainder of her portable worldly goods, but in the end decided to take them with her. The tiny refrigerator and sink would have to stay as they were fixed in place. That only left her personal papers.

Standing at the rear of the vehicle, she pulled back the carpet, poked a finger into a hole in the metal over the wheel well and pulled. A whole section the size of a cigar box came up. Reaching inside the resulting hole, she brought out the folded leather packet and tucked it into the small handbag where she'd placed the fifty bucks the doc had given her the day before. Then she paused to survey the small van that had been her home these past many weeks.

Shaking her head, she pulled the tailgate closed, saying, "I wouldn't have spent the last of my cash repairing this thing if I'd known it was going to be repossessed so soon."

"It was the right thing to do, though," he pointed out. "I mean, you had the use of the vehicle all those months without paying for it."

She gave him a droll look. "The van's worth a lot more than the six hundred bucks I owe the bank, even when you figure in the penalties."

"Six hundred dollars," he exclaimed, eyes wide. "That's all you owe? You ought to be able to earn that in a week as a medical transcriptionist."

Parking a hand on her hip, she struck a pose. "Is that a job offer, Doc? I could work for you until my stitches come out, earn enough to re-deem my van, and then I could be on my way with no worries."

He opened his mouth only to close it again and clap a hand to the back of his neck.

"You know you want me out of your hair," she pressed, fingers twirling about his head.

He didn't so much as crack a smile, so she ad-opted another tack, promising, "I'm good and fast, with a keyboard, that is." Still nothing. "I have a very high rate of transcription proficiency and, believe it or not, a gift for organization. Besides, it's not like I've got anything else to do for the next week." He just stared at her, so she folded her arms, challenging him. "Test me."

Finally, he spoke. "How do I know you're even physically able to work?"

She popped the tailgate again and crawled back into the van to open the trunk and remove a bag of prescription bottles. Tossing them to him, she slid back out onto the ground.

"I couldn't afford to refill, so I went off my meds, but if you'll help me, I'll go back on them."

He pulled apart the zipper closure and began quickly reading the prescription labels, glancing at her from time to time. "Half of these are redun-dant," he said, sounding angry.

"I know. I was trading off, seeing what worked best."

"And?"

She plucked two bottles from the bag. "This one makes me sleepy. This one upsets my stomach." She grabbed two more, holding up the first. "Sinus congestion." She tossed the second back into the bag, saying, "Keeps me awake. Otherwise, I haven't noticed many side effects or many effects, period."

"That would be the point. What about your aphasia?"

"The only other time I've ever experienced aphasia was just before my initial diagnosis."

"And then you were given intravenous drugs?"

"Yes. Just like this last time."

"And that alleviated your symptoms?"

"Exactly."

"Then, obviously you need an oral equivalent of the intravenous drug," he said.

"But that's not what you have in your hands?" she asked.

"No, not really. The intravenous medication is closely targeted. These are broader spectrum."

She nodded. "I see."

"I'll write you a new prescription," he said.

"You do that," she replied, "but if you don't give me a job, I won't be able to fill it."

He sighed, bowed his head and pressed his temples with the thumb and forefinger of one hand. "Don't worry about the prescription. As for the job, we'll go to my office now and see just what you can really do. If you're as good as you say

and if you pass a physical, I'll redeem your van
and let you work off the costs while your scalp
is healing."

Bouncing up on her tiptoes, she clapped her
hands.

"*If,*" he reminded her. "I said 'if,' and I meant
it."

She snapped him a smart salute. "Yes, sir, Doctor, sir." With that she turned and hugged her
dirty, scruffy old van.

"Get in the car," he grumbled.

Eva ran to do just that. Things were looking up,
as up as they could look for a cheeky gal with a
time bomb ticking inside her head, anyway.

Chapter Five

Maybe he was the one who needed his head examined, Brooks mused, unlocking the private entrance to his office, across the street from the hospital. He flipped on light switches as he shrugged out of his overcoat and reached into the cubbyhole that served as a closet for a hanger. As he hung his coat on the rod there, he gestured for Eva to do the same.

"Leave your—" He stopped and stared at her. "Do you even own a coat?" From what he had seen, she owned very little clothing at all.

"No," she answered blithely, folding her shawls over a hanger.

"How on earth did you survive in Kansas City without a winter coat?"

She shrugged. "I worked at home."

"You had to have had a coat at some point."

A sly smile curved her luscious lips. "I did, a fine one."

Shaking his head, he turned down the hall, beckoning her to follow, but when they got to the exam room, she balked.

"Sugar, I was born at night, but it wasn't last night. I want a job, not a physical, and I won't be denied the job because of this thing in my head without first proving I can *do* the job. Transcription test first."

Brooks sighed. "Fine. This way."

She batted her eyelashes at him. "Why, thank you."

He rolled his eyes, constantly torn between laughing and shaking her until her teeth rattled. Leading her to the office where what little on-site transcription was done, he flipped on the overhead light and gestured to the particular desk where the part-time transcriptionist sat. "I have a partner," he explained, "but we keep separate staffs and operate in different parts of the building. Right now we share a transcriptionist. There's a head-set and—"

She lifted a hand to silence him as she lowered herself onto the chair. After a quick glance around, she turned on the computer, located the foot-operated player deck and fit the headset to her head. "Any file in particular that you're needing?"

"Well, the Magruder notes need to go to the cardiologist before Friday, but—"

Again, she lifted that hand, even as she operated the computer mouse with the other. Then she began typing. Her fingers fairly flew. He stood there in the doorway, waiting for her to finish, but it soon became obvious that she wasn't just planning an exercise. She meant to finish the entire report. Brooks went to power up his own computer, then he jotted down how she was to send the file for him to proof and laid the note on the corner of the desk she was using before taking himself off to make a pot of coffee. Looked as though they were going to be there for a while. The pot was still brewing when she showed up in the break room door.

"Got a question?"

She shook her head.

"Taking a break?"

Putting her back to the doorjamb, she polished her fingernails on her shoulder and said, "I am done."

"What?"

"Done. Finished. It's all over but the proofreading."

"You can't be serious."

"As a brain tumor," she deadpanned. "Sweetie, I told you. I'm good and fast. Go see for yourself."

He pushed past her and went to his office. The message New File blinked in the corner of his computer screen. Clicking on it, he watched the file unfold, nine single-spaced pages jammed with medical acronyms and terms. Every word read correctly. She'd even fixed his grammar. He tried to speak in perfect syntax, but he was always rushed and always made mistakes. Usually, his transcriptionist typed the first draft exactly as he spoke it into the recorder, then he corrected the grammar himself during the proofreading and sent it back. Most transcription was done off-site by a service hired to handle the proofreading and corrections, including grammar and syntax. The turnaround often took weeks, however, and some cases were too time-sensitive to wait. Eva had produced the transcription as quickly as he'd recorded it, almost as quickly as he could read it.

She handed him a cup of coffee, then sat down across the desk from him to sip her own brew while he finished. He sent the file on its way, two days early, and that was a fine feeling! When he logged on to the office work chart, he checked off the transcription with his initials and hers. Afterward, he sat back and drank his coffee, contemplating the woman in front of him.

"You are good, the best I've ever seen."

She smiled. "So do I get the job?"

He just looked at her. After a moment she sighed and set her disposable coffee cup on his desk. "On to the examination room."

She got up and left the room. Smiling, he rose and followed to find her frowning at the examination table.

Hands on hips, she asked, "So should I disrobe?"

"Don't be ridiculous. With us here alone, that would be unethical."

She lifted her eyebrows at him. "Spoilsport."

"You like to be outrageous, don't you?"

"Not very."

He worked hard at not rolling his eyes. Again. "On the table."

She hopped up and dropped her shoes. He slid them out of his way with one foot and reached for the blood pressure cuff. Five minutes later, he'd examined everything he logically and ethically could under the circumstances, and if he hadn't known she had a brain tumor, he wouldn't have guessed it.

"Turn to the wall, I want to look at your stitches."

Pivoting on her hip, she swung her legs from one side of the table to another. Carefully, he parted her hair. She had skeins and skeins of the stuff, all of it silky and straight, though the closer he got to her wound the more it could use a shampooing. Still, the stitches looked surprisingly healthy, all things considered.

"I'm glad this didn't happen in the summertime," he told her. "I'd have had to shave a significantly larger section just to try to keep these stitches cooler. Perspiration has a nasty way of causing infection, and you have a thick blanket of hair here."

"Don't I know it," she told him. "Something else I can thank my mom for." She looked toward the ceiling, waved a hand and chirped, "Thanks, Mom! Thanks a million."

"Something else?" Brooks parroted.

She grabbed a hank and tugged. "The hair." Fluttering her lashes, she added, "The eyes." Pointing toward her temple with her forefinger, her hand shaped like a cocked gun, she said, "The tumor. She died of the same thing."

Brooks clasped her wrist with his hand. "I'm sorry. I didn't realize."

For once, she sobered. "It was awful. They tried everything. The chemo made her hair come out in chunks. She threw up for months, speaking gibberish half the time. She was bones in a bag of gray skin filled with agony by the time she died. When my sister got cancer, too, I wanted to die for her just to spare her the treatment."

Brooks mentally reeled. "Oh, Eva. I can't imagine. How awful for your family—three women with brain cancer."

"No, not brain cancer," she said impatiently. "Ava had breast cancer, and by the time she found the lump, it was too far gone. We were so young that Ava just didn't pay attention until it was too late."

"How old was she?"

"We were twenty-two," Eva said.

We. Twins. Eva and Ava. Suddenly, everything clicked into place. "You didn't have breast implants. You had prophylactic double mastectomy and reconstruction."

"Yep. No breast cancer for me. Should've gone for the brain implant," she quipped. "But, hey, you know what they say. Die young, leave a good-looking corpse. Well, a shapely one, anyway."

Appalled, Brooks didn't know what to do other than to lean a hip against the table and wrap an arm about her shoulders. "Eva," he said, "this is not your mother's brain tumor. Things are different now. You haven't even had a biopsy, have you?"

"I don't need one. The same doctor who diagnosed Mom diagnosed me."

"That doesn't mean your tumors are identical. Treatment has advanced significantly."

She flew off the table, rounding on him with blazing anger in her eyes. "I won't put my s—" She stopped and pinched the bridge of her nose. "I won't subject myself to what my mother went through. I have no money, no insurance, no home. I don't even have a car right now!" She folded her arms tightly, as if holding herself together. "I just want to die on my own terms. Is that too much to ask?"

"I don't know," he told her honestly. She looked away, and he made himself go on. "So far as the job is concerned, it's yours." She shot him a surprised look, so he hastened to add, "As for everything else, I have to pray about it because I just don't know."

She threw out a hip and parked a hand on it. "I'm not sure what you mean by 'everything else,' but I'll thank you for the job and my van."

"You don't have to thank me."

"I just did, though. Now this is the part where you say, 'Why, you're welcome.' Then I go clean up the break room and shut down the transcription desk like a good employee. See? There's a rhythm and routine to these things." She made a churning motion with her hands, which elicited a smile from him.

"Okay, um, I need to make a couple of phone calls then we can go."

She walked around the exam table and stepped into her shoes. For some reason that reminded him of his promise to Magnolia.

"Uh, there is one other thing," he told her. "One condition."

She looked up sharply, then her old insouciance slipped into place. "Yeah? Something fun, I hope?"

"I think so," he stated firmly, not at all sure that she would agree. "The Chatam sisters…and I…would like you to attend a meeting tonight."

Suspicion threaded her tone even as she quipped, "Brain tumors anonymous?"

"Prayer meeting."

She lifted both hands and stacked them over her forehead. *"Really?"*

"They're giving you free housing and meals, Eva. It's little enough to ask." She threw up her hands. "They believe it will help. And so do I."

Sighing dramatically, she acquiesced. "Well, I don't suppose it can actually hurt. Much."

He breathed a silent sigh of relief and took himself off to do something not quite ethical, after all. As soon as he'd called in her prescriptions, he prayed in a very concentrated manner, then he called the doctor whose name was on the original bottles, identified himself as Eva's new physician and had a chat with that elderly gentleman. The fellow was about to retire and sounded greatly relieved that Eva had found another medical provider, offering to send along her records and saying that Brooks could mail the necessary signed form later. Brooks decided that was a subject he would broach with her on another day, reasoning that it wasn't as if he'd asked for the records. Something just didn't feel right about this diagnosis, but without running tests himself, he could only check what the other doctor had done. At least he would have those records now. The rest was a matter for more prayer, as he'd told Eva earlier. Much prayer.

Prayer was to be the theme of the evening, it seemed. Eva had barely walked back through the sunny yellow door of Chatam House than the Bluebird of Happiness descended, accompanied by her Easter egg husband.

"We've been worried," Odelia confessed, wringing her hands, "wondering what was taking so long. We were praying you hadn't had a relapse."

"No, no, nothing like that," Eva rushed to tell her. "What I have is—"

To her surprise, the doc interrupted her with, "Boxes to be carried in."

"Oh, perhaps I can be of assistance," Easter Egg offered, the old gallant.

At the same time, Bluebird chirped, "I'll get Chester." She fluttered off down the hallway, adding, "Then we can try on coats!"

"Coats?" Eva echoed, only to feel Brooks's hand at her elbow, his head bent near her ear.

"Let me handle the job issue, will you please?"

He lifted a forefinger to his lips in the universal sign for silence before quickly following Kent out onto the porch. Flummoxed, Eva tilted back her head, frowning at the painted ceiling. She imagined the gates of Heaven opening just beyond and thought, *Well, why not?* Everyone else around here seemed to think prayer a perfectly normal activity.

"So, do you know what's going on here?" she asked in a conversational tone, striking a pose with one hand propped on the curled newel at the end of the staircase.

"Of course, I do," said a voice quite close behind her.

Eva jumped, whirling to find Magnolia smiling up at her. "Penny Loafers, you scared fifteen minutes off my life," she declared, slapping a hand to her chest, "and I really haven't got 'em to spare."

Nodding, Magnolia pulled in a deep breath. "We feared as much."

"Uh, the Kindred Spirit mentioned something about coats."

Magnolia put on a thin smile. "Indeed. We thought the ballroom would be the best place for that." She beckoned with her hand. "Follow me."

Off they went down the far hallway, past the library and music room to an honest-to-goodness ballroom, where double pocket doors stood open.

"Wow." Eva stuck her nose inside, intent on taking it all in, only to draw up short when she came to a rolling rack of clothing—coats, to be exact. Surprised to see that the other two sisters, seated on matching lyre-back chairs, seemed to be waiting for her to join them, she stepped through the door, overcome with curiosity. "What gives?"

Silk-and-Pearls smiled. "Odelia mentioned that you are lacking an adequate winter coat, so we've gathered several we think might suit you."

Eva strode farther into the cavernous room, focusing on the rack of garments. "You call this a few?"

Hypatia spread her hands. "Without knowing

your size, we felt it necessary to err on the side of excess."

Odelia clapped, urging, "Choose some and try them on."

Torn between wanting to play along and sheer pride, Eva dithered. She wandered over to the rack and took the first garment from the hanger, a double-breasted gray wool, which proved too small, as did a brown nylon car coat and military-style bomber jacket. The fashion show went on, however. She tried on a long navy trench coat with short sleeves, a frumpy tweed that swallowed her, a silky belted job that felt like a bathrobe and a bright yellow raincoat with a zip-out liner. So it went until she'd worked her way through the whole collection. The most workable was a shiny black vinyl, three-quarter length A-line with a wide brown faux fur collar and cuffs.

Then there was the cape, a completely impractical off-white wool lined with some silky fabric that swirled around her ankles and made her feel like a medieval princess, especially with the hood up and the metal fastener closed at her throat. She lusted after that cape. It was *so* classy. She glanced around the ballroom and reasoned that it must be affecting her judgment for she could suddenly see herself with her hair up, and of course she wore a gorgeous gown and clung to the arm of...

No way. She wasn't going there. Every other female in Buffalo Creek, Texas, could hanker after Doc Gorgeous, but she wasn't going to be one of the throng ever again. Even if she had a future to waste on such stupidity, she'd learned her lesson the hard way. The guy that all the girls wanted was also the guy who got all the girls he wanted—and he lied when he told you that he'd only ever want you.

Regretfully, she took off the cape and returned it to the rack. "I'll take the vinyl with the fur collar."

The sisters traded looks. Hypatia crossed her ankles and tucked them beneath her chair.

"If you don't mind my saying so, the cape suits you better."

"You have very long arms," Odelia pointed out.

Eva held out the offending appendages. "No! Really? I hadn't noticed." She made a show of looking over her arms then winked and said, "Actually, the only coat I've ever owned that truly fit me was made for me, a luscious red fox. My ex gave it to me, then he pawned it, but I found the ticket and redeemed it then sold it for the down payment on my van."

Again, the sisters did that glance-glance thing. Eva parked her hands at her waist. "What is that? Some sort of mindreading thing you three do? It's like you talk without speaking."

Magnolia chuckled. "When you've lived together as long as we have, you hardly have to speak to know what the others are thinking."

"Yeah? And that would be?"

Magnolia folded her arms. "You should take both the coat and the cape. Provided..." She glanced at her sisters again.

Eva copied her pose. "Provided what, Penny Loafers?"

"Provided you attend prayer meeting tonight after dinner."

Dropping her hands to her hips again, Eva cocked a knee. "Boy, you dames don't mind employing a little manipulation, do you?"

Hypatia cleared her throat.

"Oh, don't give me that silent scolding, Miss Silk-and-Pearls," Eva said. "I'll go to your precious prayer meeting, for all the good it'll do." Turning on her heel, she snatched the coat and the cape from the rack, hangers and all, as she strode for the door, only to find the doc lounging there against the jamb, his own arms folded.

"Actually," he drawled, "it's a toss up as to who might be doing the manipulating here, as you have already made a deal with *me* to attend prayer meeting tonight."

"No," she said sweetly, sauntering past him, "it's only a matter of who the better manipulator might be."

"No comment," he rumbled.

"I would think not," she returned, blissfully aware that he watched as she sashayed, literally, down that hall, "considering what *you* traded for my attendance."

"Dinner in half an hour," Magnolia called behind her. Eva lifted a hand in acknowledgment, hearing the old girl say, "You'll join us, won't you, Brooks dear?"

"Absolutely," he replied.

Eva smiled, even as she felt the scorching heat of his gaze on her back. She knew that she was lucky to escape without being burned to a cinder and that antagonizing him was foolish, all things considered, but at this point she only had so much to lose.

After stowing her things, she changed into clean clothes, choosing the skirt, a T-shirt and a shawl with which to disguise it, along with her cowboy boots. Then she brushed her hair into a ponytail caught against the nape of her neck, took her new coat and handbag and went downstairs, ready for dinner. She found the doc awaiting her in the parlor. He rose to his feet when she entered.

"I was about to come looking for you."

"Whatever for?"

"The aunties are punctual about the dinner hour, especially on Wednesdays."

"I'm not late."

"You're not early," he said, turning her by the arm back into the foyer. He took her handbag and hung it by the strap over the newel post, slung her coat over that and caught her hand, towing her down the hallway on the left side of the staircase and through the door of a large dark room with ugly wallpaper and an enormous table surrounded by heavy chairs. Even the fireplace was fronted by heavy, dark wood.

The sisters and Kent were all seated at one end and on one side of the table, so that everyone but Hypatia had their backs to the door. They craned their necks to peer around or over the backs of their chairs as Brooks shook free of Eva's hand. She glared at him—she hadn't grabbed him, after all—and smiled at the others.

"What's on the preprayer meeting menu?"

Odelia blinked owlishly, but the Easter Egg answered, "Beef and barley soup and soda bread."

"Smells great."

She followed Brooks around the table and reached for a chair, only to realize that he had pulled out one for her. Affecting her best lady-of-the-manor manner, she lifted her chin, slid onto the seat and gave him a nasally, "Thenk ewe, my good man."

He gave her back an impatient glance and took the chair between her and Hypatia, snapping his linen napkin open across his lap. Eva spread hers and reached for a slice of the steaming soda bread. At the same time, Hypatia cleared her throat, rather violently, and Brooks dropped a quelling hand on Eva's knee.

"Oops," Eva quipped, withdrawing her hand. "Pre-preprayer meeting meal prayer. Right?"

"Something like that," Magnolia muttered.

At the same time, Brooks leaned over and whispered, "Behave."

"Relax," she muttered out of the side of her mouth, bowing her head. Kent voiced a wordy prayer over the meal. As soon as he said, "Amen," she slapped Brooks's hand away and reached for the soda bread.

"Mmm-mmm. Smells delish. Either that or I'm starved. Or both. Hey, what is soda bread, anyway?"

"Obviously, it's bread made with soda instead of yeast or baking powder," Brooks told her as Odelia began ladling thick dark soup into bowls from the large tureen on the table.

"It's an Irish recipe, I believe," Hypatia added.

Chester came into the room just then, carrying a plate of deviled eggs and pickled beets, which he placed in front of Kent. He returned a minute later to set in front of Eva a steaming deep-dish apple pie and cheese board.

She looked up at him and said with all solemnity and seriousness, "I adore your wife."

"Well, that makes it unanimous," announced Brooks.

"I'm warning you now," Eva said, taking her filled soup bowl, "I'm going to pack a lunch to work, and if I catch you stealing it, I'll prosecute."

She didn't realize until she'd dipped her spoon and was blowing on the rich dark soup in preparation for eating it that the table had gone completely still and silent. Only then did she realize what she'd said. Grimacing, she dropped the spoon back into the bowl.

Brooks sighed and said, "It turns out that Eva is a gifted medical transcriptionist, so she's going to work for me temporarily."

A veritable chorus of "Oh, dears" went around the table.

Hypatia reached for his hand, while Penny Loafers frowned at Eva, and Odelia leaned against her husband, who wrapped a comforting arm around her plump shoulders.

"Brooks, dear, are you sure about this?" Hypatia asked, her brow furrowed.

All Eva could think was that they feared for her health, so she shrugged, and said, "Hey, I won't be typing with my skull. It'll be fine. Really."

They ignored her to a person, all eyes fixed on Brooks.

He squeezed Hypatia's hand, spread a smile around the table and said, "Dear hearts, I'm forty-four years old. I think I can manage this, but bless you all for loving me enough to be so concerned."

"You're like one of our own, you know," Hypatia told him in a shaky voice.

"I know. I count on it."

"We just want you to be happy."

"I am happy."

"We want you to stay that way," Magnolia stated bluntly, glancing at Eva.

"Hey," Eva said, "I'm really good at what I do. It's not like I'm going to mess things up."

To her utter consternation, his hand landed on her knee again. She snapped at him. "Will you cut that out?"

"Will you pipe down?" he shot back. Taking his hand from her knee, he added, more sedately, "Eat your soup."

She shook her head, aware that she was missing something, but too hungry and confused to care at the moment. Sitting forward again, she started to eat. The soup was very good, though she'd never before eaten barley, and the soda bread was even better, especially with butter. The pie, though, defied description, especially with the cheese melting on top of it.

"Mmm," she hummed, waving her fork over it, "the next time you want me to go to prayer meeting, just promise me this pie. I am now officially a pie wh—er, hog." She slid a look at Brooks out of the corner of her eye and found him pinching the bridge of his nose. "Interior monitor," she muttered.

"Is a little slow."

She shrugged and shoveled in another bite. "But on the job."

"Uh-huh."

After licking her fork, she dropped it to the plate and pushed the plate away, then sighed happily. "So," she asked, "am I going to have to confess my gluttony at this prayer meeting of yours?"

The sisters traded exasperated looks and began getting to their feet.

"Of course not," Magnolia said.

"We're going to pray for your health," Odelia told her brightly.

"Oh, well, that and two bucks will get me a cup of coffee. Somewhere. Probably."

Brooks sighed, and Hypatia announced briskly, "It's time we were going."

"You go on," he said. "Eva will ride with me."

The poor old thing looked almost stricken. "Are you sure?"

"Trust me," he said, nodding.

She looked at Eva before turning away. "We'll see you there."

"We're right behind you," Brooks promised, but when Eva moved to stand, he slammed that hand down on her knee again.

"What is your prob—" she began, but he quelled her with a squeeze of his hand, nothing painful, just enough to let her know that he wanted her to shut up. She counted to ten, picturing her van in her mind's eye to remind herself why she should bite her tongue.

As soon as the oldsters exited the room, he was in her face, nose to nose with her. "Listen," he said softly but firmly, "you may not believe, and that's fine, but they do, and I won't have you making fun of their faith, not after the generosity and concern they've shown you."

"I was just joking," she defended weakly, knowing he was right.

"You were just sneering. Cut it out or you can forget the job and the van and, if I have anything to say about it, the room and everything else."

Ashamed, Eva bowed her head. "I didn't mean to sneer. Truly I didn't, but I don't get what's going on here. What's the issue with the job? That's not charity. That's honest employment. You'll see. I'll do good work for you, I promise."

"Don't swear," he snapped. "Just behave yourself and be respectful."

"I didn't mean to be disrespectful," she told him, "and I don't think that's the problem. It's almost as if they're afraid of me somehow."

He rubbed a hand over his head and said, "They're concerned for *me*, Eva. They know that I'm attracted to you, and they don't want to see me hurt."

Some seconds ticked by before she realized that her mouth was hanging open. They *knew* that he was attracted to her? And they didn't want him hurt. The implications of this both elated and deeply saddened her.

She shook her head, reminding herself why a romance with Doc Gorgeous—or any man—

was impossible, gulped and said, "B-because I'm dying, you mean."

He looked her in the eye then, and she thought, she just knew, that he was going to say something incredibly heroic and stupid like, "You're not going to die," or "I won't let you die."

Instead, he got to his feet and said, "Because my wife was dying when I married her."

Then he walked out and left her sitting there with her mouth hanging open again.

Chapter Six

Rendering Eva speechless for once proved strangely pleasurable for Brooks. She said not a word all the way to the church. After they left the car and walked toward the chapel on the sprawling campus of the Downtown Bible Church, she obviously became more and more uncomfortable. He could literally see her shoulders tighten and her head sink lower as her steps grew shorter. He wondered what she expected, a public pillory?

His own spirits stuttered when he pulled open the heavily carved door and found Morgan and Lyla in the foyer. Mentally cringing during the introductions, he braced himself for Eva's first quip. Instead, she seemed to have eyes only for Bri.

"Ooohhh, she's adorable."

"We think so," Lyla admitted. Bri reached out to grab a tiny fistful of Eva's fur collar.

"Her little hands are just perfect. I love baby fingers."

"I know. Aren't they sweet?"

"I remember," Eva began, only to shake her head.

Brooks realized suddenly that she had choked up. It hit him all at once that she was unlikely ever to know the joy of having her own child and that she must feel that loss keenly. All at once, she reached behind her and flipped her ponytail over onto Bri's head. The blond shades weren't so far apart, but Bri still had little hair to cover her tender skull.

"Preview!" Eva sang, arranging the wisps of hair atop Bri's head. "The girl's gonna be a knockout."

Lyla Simone laughed as Bri tried to pull Eva's hair down over her face. "Won't be long until you have your own ponytail," she promised.

"Don't rush it," Morgan pleaded. "She was a newborn just yesterday, and now she's walking. The next thing we know it'll be ponytails and bicycles."

"Then driving," Eva drawled, adding sound effects to approximate screeching tires and revving engines. Morgan clutched his chest.

Even as Brooks laughed, he realized that Eva used her humor and outrageousness to fight fear and dismay. He didn't know why he hadn't seen it sooner, perhaps because he wasn't convinced that her prognosis was the correct one. Whatever he suspected, however, Eva believed she was dying of a brain tumor, and that had to be terrifying, especially for a woman alone in a strange place.

Frowning, he wondered how that had come to be. He knew that her mother and sister had already died, but did she have no other family? No one who could convince her to have a proper workup of tests done and take an honest look at her situation? What about friends? Surely she had friends. Someone somewhere must care about this woman.

They followed Morgan into the cross-shaped sanctuary, while Lyla Simone hurried off to the nursery with Bri. The Chatam sisters had saved chairs for them in the front of the central section. They filed into place, leaving the aisle seat for Lyla, who slipped into place just before the pastor stepped up to the microphone at the center of the space.

They began with a hymn. Then the pastor read a Scripture selection. Next, volunteers passed out printed sheets with prayer requests while the pastor asked if anyone had a personal petition to add to the list.

Magnolia rose, laid her hand on Eva's shoulder and said in a firm voice, "Our friend Eva is in need of healing." With that, she sat down again.

Around them, pens clicked and scribbling commenced as Eva's name was added to the list. Others spoke their concerns. Eventually heavy accordion curtains closed off the four sections of the sanctuary, and a leader rose in each one to lead the participants of the four groups in prayer. Morgan led their particular group. Quite a few prayed aloud. Brooks chose not to speak, but he prayed silently for Eva's physical, emotional and spiritual healing, as well as all the other requests. He couldn't help noticing, however, that Eva merely sat quietly, staring down at her hands.

At the end of the hour, the dividers were pushed back, and the congregation joined together for a few announcements, a closing hymn and a benediction. Then they were free to depart, though most hung around to chat for a while. Eva nodded and smiled at those who wished her well. Before the Chatam sisters could suggest that she ride back to the house with them, Brooks walked her out to his car and opened the passenger door for her, curious about her impressions of the prayer meeting. He didn't have long to wait.

No sooner did he slide behind the steering wheel than she erupted with, "Doesn't it make you angry when God fails to heal the sick?"

Stunned, he turned to her. "Angry?"

"You're a doctor! You're all about healing. If you really believe in God, then you must believe that He has the ability to heal."

"I do."

"Then, why aren't you savagely angry that He doesn't do it?" she demanded.

Brooks shifted in his seat, marshaling his thoughts. "Eva, no one has a *right* to healing, any more than we have a right to forgiveness. These are gifts from God, products of His grace, showered on this fallen world. His forgiveness is there for anyone willing to ask for it, but healing, like so many other blessings, is received as God wills, and we can't always know why He chooses one action over another. God might choose to heal one of His children by taking him or her home to Heaven, for reasons known only to God at the time. As wrong as it may seem to us, we can trust that God always chooses the action that is best for all concerned, because He, and He alone, can truly see the future and the needs of all involved."

"But you try to cure disease yourself," she argued.

"Yes, and I will go on trying," he stated flatly, "because that is my calling, but I never forget that ultimate healing is God's work alone. I don't understand why some must suffer horribly while others enjoy great good health until the day God calls them home, but I know that it is never without reason, that my job is to alleviate the suffering as much as humanly possible and that God always answers prayer—even if the answer isn't always what I'd like it to be."

Eva frowned. "You're saying that *death* is a kind of healing."

"For the Christian, yes."

"And you think I'm cuckoo for coconuts," she drawled, rolling her eyes.

He shook his head. "No, I don't. What I think, what I believe, is that this world and this life were never meant to be permanent, and for Christians, death is just the door to eternity, which will be spent in Heaven, where there will be no illness. Ever. If that's not healing, I don't know what is."

While she considered that, the Chatam sisters and Kent came strolling down the sidewalk toward the town car. Just before they drew alongside his vehicle, Hypatia stumbled on a perfectly level pavement and went to her knees, catching herself on the heels of her hands. Brooks yanked open his car door and leaped out, reaching her before the others got over their shock well enough to react.

"Hypatia?"

He could see that she was panting and trembling, her face pale in the light of the streetlamp. Easing her onto one hip, he laid the back of his hand against her forehead, finding it cool and clammy. Quickly, he checked her pulse, which was rapid but slowing.

"S-silly of me."

She shivered violently, her head jerking to one side.

"Let's get you off this cold ground," Brooks said, rising and taking her with him, his hands fixed firmly beneath her arms. She seemed to weigh little more than a bird, but then she'd always been small. Still, she seemed brittle, fragile somehow. He turned her toward the town car, walking slowly and carefully. "All right?"

"Yes. Thank you." She lifted a hand to her hair, as if a strand of it would dare to fall out of place. "I feel so foolish, tripping like that."

Brooks glanced behind them, and saw nothing whatsoever to cause anyone to trip. "I'd like you to come in for a checkup," he told her, keeping his voice light. He didn't realize that Eva had come to help until she opened the car door for Hypatia, who smiled and nodded.

"Yes, dear. If you say so."

"It would put my mind at ease."

She reached up and patted his cheek. "I'll call tomorrow."

He bent down and kissed her forehead. "I look forward to it."

Kent had handed Odelia down into the front passenger seat and come around to the driver's side, while Magnolia had come to stand next to Eva. "Perhaps you'll help us get Hypatia home," she suggested, patting Eva's shoulder. As Hypatia slid to the center of the backseat, Eva sent Brooks an amused look, then nodded and got inside.

"I'll pick you up for work at seven-thirty in the morning," Brooks said to Eva before closing the door and walking over to open the other side for Magnolia.

Hypatia reached out a hand to him. "Join us for breakfast," she invited.

Smiling, he said, "I'll do that." Then he backed up and closed the door, happy enough to have Eva off his hands for a while, despite the unsettling episode with Hypatia. He forgot sometimes that the aunties were growing older. Now if only he could forget Eva Belle Russell for ten hours or so.

Despite a restless night, Eva rose early the next morning and dressed with care. She looped her long hair in a heavy, sleek bun at the nape of her neck, then added dark mascara and a touch of shiny translucent red lip gloss. She told herself that she wanted to make a good impression on the other employees, but certain words kept running through her mind.

They know I'm attracted to you. They know I'm attracted to you...

The whole thing was insane, of course. Even if he *were* attracted to her, he wouldn't act on it. Why would he given her condition, his past and the fact that he doubtlessly had to do little more than snap his fingers to have women falling all over him? Yet, she swabbed on that lip gloss.

Not only that shocking after-dinner revelation had kept her tossing and turning, however. Little Bri Chatam had nearly brought Eva to her knees, so like Ricky was she. Oh, he'd nearly grown up now, but his baby pictures would show a virtual twin to Morgan and Lyla Simone's little girl. Eva had found herself near tears, swamped with memories of those halcyon days when she'd still believed that her husband actually loved her and they would grow old together, raising their son to adulthood. She'd even dared to plan a second child.

Most disturbing of all the events that had kept her awake through the night, though, had been the prayer meeting. Her aunt's church went in for a much more demonstrative and emotional kind of service, with the pastor demanding that folks publicly confess their sins and that evil spirits come out of them. Eva had heard some hair-curling confessions at those meetings, but she'd never heard her aunt confess her meanness and hypercriticism. All that had happened last night was that people had prayed for others, sometimes simply, sometimes eloquently but always sincerely and quietly. She'd felt a strange power in that place, as well as an inexplicable kind of peace, and yet, illness and trouble remained. She had no doubt of that!

So what was the point? Brooks's comments to her in the car after the meeting kept playing through her head. *No one has a right to healing. His forgiveness is there for anyone willing to ask for it, but healing...is received as God wills... We can trust that God always chooses the action that is best for all concerned...* She didn't understand it all, but his words woke a kind of longing in her that she couldn't quite identify—and she worked so hard not to want what she couldn't have. She often exhausted herself trying not to want what she couldn't have.

Dressed to meet the day, she went downstairs, hung her handbag and coat on the newel post at the bottom of the steps, and hurried to the sunroom for a breakfast sumptuous enough to make Eva weep with joy. Odelia and Kent were already at the table. Brooks showed up right after the coffee with Eva's prescriptions, three bottles of pills, one to be taken with meals, one at bedtime, one in the morning on an empty stomach. Magnolia came in on the doctor's handsome heels. They were halfway through the meal before Brooks wondered aloud what could be keeping Hypatia.

"I've never known her to sleep in."

Magnolia snorted primly. "I expect she rose early and has already eaten, trying to prove how hale she is after last night's little mishap."

"No," Hilda said, coming into the room with a basket of fresh biscuits. "She hasn't come to the table yet."

Brooks frowned around the table. "Has anyone checked on her?"

Magnolia's brow furrowed. "I'll go."

No sooner had she left the room, however, than Brooks tossed his napkin onto the table, saying, "I don't like this. Not after that fall last night."

Odelia looked troubled. "She has seemed…not herself lately."

Brooks shot to his feet and took off after Magnolia. Odelia glanced worriedly at her husband and went after Brooks, Kent lumbering along behind her. Dropping her fork, Eva followed, catching the unmistakable whiff of alarm. By the time she reached the head of the stairs, she could hear Magnolia shrieking for Brooks, who had already disappeared. Eva hurried after Odelia and Kent, resisting the urge to push past them through the door to the suite shared by the sisters. She skirted them in the sitting room, somewhat surprised by its comfortable shabbiness, and strode boldly into the small bedroom where Magnolia stood with her hands clapped to her face, staring at the floor.

Brooks knelt there over a crumpled Hypatia, who looked tiny and fragile in navy silk pajamas piped in ivory, her long, silver hair caught at her nape in a ponytail coming undone while she gasped for breath, her lips a ghastly blue, her eyes open but dull and unseeing. Brooks held her limp wrist while staring at his watch. After a few seconds, he looked up.

"Kent, we need chewable aspirin. I have it in my bag in the car if there's none in the house. Eva, dial 9-1-1. Use the phone on the bedside table. Don't hang up. I need to speak with dispatch personally."

Kent hurried from the room at a trot. Eva slipped around to the bedside table and lifted the telephone receiver. Hypatia whispered something then. Brooks leaned close, listened and nodded.

"Yes, dear, I know. I'm going to lift you onto the bed now."

The emergency operator came on the line. "9-1-1. What is your emergency?"

Eva drew a blank for a moment, then stammered, "O-one of the Chatams h-has collapsed. Dr. Leland wants an ambulance a-at Chatam House right away."

The operator, a woman, didn't even ask for an address. Instead, she said, "Your name?"

"Eva Russell." Brooks had scooped up Hypatia and carefully laid her on the bed. Now he held out a hand for the telephone receiver. Eva said, "Hang on. Dr. Leland wants to speak to you." Then she gave him the cordless receiver.

He stepped into the corner and turned his back to the room, speaking softly. While he did so, Odelia and Magnolia huddled together, alternately staring at him and Hypatia, their lips moving in silent prayer. Hypatia, meanwhile, panted weakly upon the narrow four-poster bed. Frightened for her, Eva stepped close and reached for Hypatia's hand. To her surprise and relief, the fingers that immediately clasped hers contained a ropy strength. Eva squeezed, and Hypatia's blue lips curved slightly.

Encouraged, Eva leaned forward and whispered, "It's okay. Brooks is here. He'll take care of everything."

Hypatia's eyes slitted open.

Taking heart, Eva quipped, "You picked a good time. The doc was in the house." Using her free hand, she flipped Hypatia a thumbs up. Hypatia's lips quirked, and she turned her free hand so that her thumb pointed up.

Kent returned then. Brooks hung up the phone, took the pill bottle and began poking tablets into Hypatia's mouth with the instruction to chew. Eva let go of her hand and went into the bathroom for a glass of water. When she returned, Brooks helped her lift up enough to drink, then he asked Eva to sit with her while he took Magnolia, Odelia and Kent into the other room. They returned mere moments later. Tears dripped from Odelia's eyes, and Magnolia looked decidedly grim. Chester arrived with Brooks's medical bag, then left to let in the emergency personnel. Brooks performed a quick examination.

Hypatia seemed to be resting more comfortably when the ambulance arrived just minutes later. Brooks stood by like a benign overseer while the technicians did their work. As soon as the gurney cleared the suite, followed by the Chatam sisters and Kent, Brooks took Eva aside on the landing.

"It's almost certainly her heart."

"I thought that might be it when you asked for the aspirin."

"I have to warn you that the family is going to be descending. Chester will have already called her brothers, and they'll be alerting the others."

Eva nodded. "How many are there?"

Brooks blew out a breath. "Lots. The thing is, normally Chester and Hilda would take care of everything, but they love Hypatia as much as the rest of us, and I'm afraid Hilda won't bear up very well. Her sister Carol, the maid, will try to take up the slack, but it could get crazy around here. You may just want to hide out in your room."

Eva lifted her eyebrows. She hadn't even known there was a maid, and she wasn't the hiding sort. Well, not really.

"Don't worry about me," she said. "Just take care of Silk-and-Pearls."

He smiled, despite the worry in his golden eyes, and started for the stairs. "I'd better get going. I want to see her again before they put her on the helicopter."

She kept pace with him as he headed down the stairs. "Helicopter?"

"It's standing by to airlift her into Dallas. Standard procedure for serious heart cases."

"I see."

"Tell the family I'll call as soon as I know anything," he said when they reached the bottom step, "but warn them that it could be hours."

"Will do."

They crossed the foyer to the front door, which he pulled open, then he paused with the blustery January breeze whipping into the house. The ambulance pulled away, its tires crunching in the deep gravel of the long looping drive. Chester had brought the town car around and was dropping down behind the wheel. Presumably Odelia and Kent sat in the back. As the car started up and drove off after the ambulance, Brooks paused and turned an agonized face to Eva.

"I love that old woman," he said softly, urgently. "I don't want to lose her." He closed his glistening eyes. "Please, God," he whispered. "We still need her." Then he sucked in a deep breath and strode purposefully through the door, pulling it closed behind him.

Eva laid her palm against it, wishing she could comfort him and everyone else who cared about Hypatia Chatam. She hated to think how he, how they all, would suffer if Hypatia died. Who, Eva wondered, would grieve her when she died? It seemed kindest, easiest, just to disappear to spare her son the angst and pain of watching her suffer, but to be unmourned…

She pushed the thought away. What mattered now was the Chatams. She just didn't realize then how vast the Chatam family was or how many people truly cared about Hypatia. She began to get a clue when the phone began to ring…and ring and ring and ring…

After countless calls, she got a question she couldn't answer from someone named Petra. She promised to have Hilda call straight away, hung up and went in search of the cook, only to find the poor woman in the kitchen, sobbing hysterically into her apron. After wrapping her arms around Hilda, Eva calmed the rotund woman as best she could, relating how Hypatia had smiled, squeezed her hand and given her a thumbs-up while waiting for the ambulance. Sniffing hopefully, her round face tear-ravaged, Hilda looked up at that.

"She was conscious, then?"

"Oh, yes. The whole time."

Hilda pulled in a shuddering breath. "Well, that's something."

"Yes, it's very good, and with the doc here in the house, her timing couldn't have been better. Right?"

Hilda straightened. "That's true." She pressed her hands together. "I should've seen it. God be praised! He had it all in place from the beginning." She let out a sigh of relief, closed her eyes and said, "Thank You, Jesus."

Eva drew back. "Uh, someone named Petra called to ask if anyone had reached the twins."

Hilda hopped to her feet in a jiggle of abundant flesh. "Oh, my! They'll all be coming. The whole lot! Where will we put them all?" She waddled to the cabinet and took a notebook and pencil from a drawer, returning quickly to the table. "All seven from California will have to stay here," she said, jotting down names. "And there'll be three—no! Four—from Stephenville. Oh, the baby's new-born, not a week old, but Chandler won't stay away, and he won't leave them behind, I just know it! The twins can have the East Suite, and we'll put Chandler, Bethany, Matthew and the baby in the Small Suite. The cradle will need to be moved into the bedroom there. It'll be crowded, but it's the best solution with Hypatia gone to…" She bit her suddenly quivering lip and bent over the notebook, scribbling away.

"Just tell me where to find the cradle," Eva offered bravely. "I'm a cradle grabber from way back, which is not to be confused with a cradle robber."

That got her a wan smile, at least. After a bit of sniffing, Hilda spoke again. "Dorinda, Tony, Melinda, JW and Johnny can stay in the Master Suite, and we'll have an extra bedroom there if it's needed, but I expect Murdock and Maryanne will want to stay with Asher, anyway. They have since Mary Ella was born." She added wryly, "They'd cram in with Phillip and his wild bunch but with Carissa expecting their fourth, that house is bursting at the seams."

"These Chatams are a lusty lot," Eva observed.

"They're the salt of the earth!" Hilda retorted defensively, "every one of them, and they deserve all the happiness this world has to offer, Hypatia especially. She deserves to get to see her great nieces and nephews be born. She…"

Eva slid an arm around Hilda's round shoulders, saying gently, "Tell me how I can help."

Chapter Seven

Hilda sent Eva to haul two enormous hams and a large beef roast from the freezer, all of which had been frozen cooked. If she was correct, the entire family, at least thirty individuals, would soon be descending upon them, so they had no time to lose.

Chester returned from the hospital, saying that Kent had dropped him off and kept the car. He fetched the cradle from the attic, and came back downstairs in time to let in a lovely young woman who introduced herself to Eva as Jessa Lynn Willows. She brought her own apron and immediately pitched in with the food preparation, saying, "Garrett and the kids will be over after they close the shops." Hilda chuckled about Garrett managing a plant nursery, floral shop and a baby on his own, but Jessa said that he was better at it than she was and that Hunter, who was ten and could close up either shop on his own, would be able to help his dad after school.

The previously unseen Carol, Hilda's sister and the maid, came in to say that all the beds had clean sheets on them and the laundry was underway. She, too, put on an apron and went to work. Her red-rimmed eyes told Eva that she had been weeping in private, but she was as quiet and unobtrusive as a mouse. Eva didn't have the heart to tease her. When Jessa asked what Eva's connection was to the family, she replied that she was working for Dr. Leland and temporarily staying at Chatam House. Jessa patted her shoulder.

"Been here, done that," she said, smiling. "How I met my husband. Garrett was the gardener here."

"Oh?"

"Mmm-hmm. The Chatam sisters have been like family to us. Technically they are family. My sister-in-law is married to Chandler Chatam, one of the nephews."

"Oh."

Soon the Petra from the telephone showed up, blonde and pretty, with her husband, Dale. Both wore jeans and work shirts along with worried expressions. "Any news?"

Before Chester could reply in the negative, the phone rang, and he left with Petra to answer it. Morgan, Lyla and Bri arrived, followed at once by Morgan's sister Kaylie and their elderly father, Hubner, older brother of the Chatam sisters.

Kaylie's husband, Stephen, had stayed at home with their newborn son, Stephen Chatam Gallow, dubbed "Chat" by the family. Hubner reported that his eldest son, Bayard, and his daughter-in-law Chloe were at the hospital in Dallas, where they lived, with Magnolia, Odelia and Kent. Bayard's daughters, Julia and Carolyn, would be splitting their time between their Dallas homes and Buffalo Creek.

Asher and Phillip, Petra's brothers, arrived with their wives, Ellie and Carissa, respectively. Ellie, who turned out to be Kent's granddaughter, had in tow her and Asher's toddler, Marie Ella. Carissa reported that her "crew" were in school until 3:00 p.m. Between the news and trying to keep all of the Chatams straight, Eva's head was swimming. Hilda banished them all from the kitchen to the family parlor, which is where Chester and Petra delivered the news that Hypatia had, indeed, suffered a major heart attack and was currently undergoing tests.

When Eva and Chester rolled a pair of tea trolleys into the room twenty minutes later, they were every one on their knees. Chester stopped just inside the door and bowed his head, but Eva stared until Hubner Chatam rose on the arm of his son, Morgan, to sink onto a comfortable armchair. This family prayed more than any she'd ever seen, but Eva couldn't deny that a sense of peace now permeated the room.

When she returned to the kitchen, she found Hilda, Jessa and Carol in fevered discussion about lunch and dinner menus.

Jessa shook her head. "You'll kill yourself trying to cook three meals a day for the entire family, Hilda."

"Needs must," Hilda insisted dismissively.

"Or," Eva ventured, "you could lay out a substantial buffet in the dining room and just keep it replenished with whatever you have on hand. Start with lunch, and after that, people can eat whenever they're hungry. You wouldn't have to worry about menus."

Hilda stared at her like she'd grown an extra eye, but Carol and Jenna smiled.

"I'll get the chafing dishes," Carol announced decisively.

Hilda parked her hands in the general vicinity of her hips and turned a circle, as if taking stock of her kitchen. "That might work," she finally allowed.

"The ham's starting to smell good," Eva said, aware suddenly that she'd missed breakfast. "Don't suppose you have any of those scrumptious muffins around, do you?"

Hilda beamed and went for the basket.

Family members and friends, many from the church, including the pastor, came and went during that busy morning. When the buffet was finally laid out in the dining room, Eva walked toward the family parlor to let everyone know. Before she reached that room, however, she saw through the window in the back door that her van was arriving. It stopped beneath what the family called the "porte cochere" at the side of the house. Stunned, she ran down the hall and threw open the door, watching as Brooks slid from the driver's seat, jogged around the front of the vehicle, climbed the few brick steps and came inside.

"You brought my van!" she squealed at him, backing up as he pushed the door closed.

He gave her a brief smile, shrugging out of his overcoat. "I'll be keeping the keys for now, though."

That seemed reasonable, considering their deal.

"But you redeemed it already," she gushed.

"I said I would."

"If I worked for you."

"And you will."

She wanted to jump up and down in delight, though she knew this wasn't the time or the place. She tried patting his chest, smiling so widely that her cheeks hurt, and found herself up on her toes. He made a sort of snuffling chuckle, a muffled sound that was part gentle derision and part pleasure, and she couldn't stop herself from throwing her arms around his neck. Then, quite without meaning to, she kissed him, hard and fast on the mouth. His smile faded into something serious and fraught with equal parts longing and sadness.

She dropped her arms and jumped back, feeling burned and embarrassed and full of forbidden desires.

They know I'm attracted to you.

"Um, do you want lunch? Hilda's put out a buffet."

He nodded. "Sounds good, but I need to speak to everyone first. Would you make sure they're all in the parlor?"

Eva nodded and hurried back to the kitchen to tell Hilda, Carol and Jessa that Brooks would like to see them in the family parlor. She followed them back there but hung in the doorway, while Brooks gave them the news.

"Hypatia is receiving the very best possible care, and she is in stable condition, resting comfortably, but she needs bypass surgery, and she's just too weak for it right now. We have to regulate her heartbeat first and get her blood oxygen levels up. That's going to take a few days, and in the interim, I'm going to ask you all to stay away from the hospital and let her rest. Meanwhile, your prayers will work wonders because, as you know, God hears and answers in the way that is best for all. Now, I'm told that Hilda has prepared a buffet in the dining room, so I suggest we all eat and go about our business."

Hubner asked Brooks if he would say a blessing before they went into the dining room, and he readily agreed. Lifting his arms about chest high and turning his palms up, he bowed his head and spoke quietly and simply.

As the family filed out, they took the time to ask quick questions and receive answers and re-assurance, until finally Brooks stood alone in the center of the room as if bolted to the floor. Eva wandered toward him.

"Are you okay?"

He looked at her, his vulnerability plain to see. "I'm not sure. Frankly I've always felt that Hypatia was somehow indomitable, unshakeable, and it's a little frightening to realize that's not the case. I'm just realizing, too, how much I've leaned on her throughout my lifetime, and it's demoralizing to find that I'm not as strong, perhaps, as I thought I was. They're all a bit eccentric, you know, the sisters, but completely adorable, and they have such enormous capacities to love and to give that it's so easy to become dependent on them. Now, suddenly, I'm not sure I measure up to their standard, and how will I ever if they're not all here to show me the way? I feel like a lost boy, like I haven't quite grown up, and I want to tell God that I'll behave like a big boy now if He just won't take Hypatia. It's…depressing, sad, awkward." He looked down at his feet, sliding his hands into the pockets of his slacks.

"You love her," Eva summed up simply.

"She's been mother, aunt, grandmother, friend,

counselor, teacher to me. They all have, at one time or another. I don't want to lose her, any of them."

Eva slid her arm through his. "I envy you that relationship."

He turned his head and stared at her. Then he smiled. "You should. It's a very great blessing. By the way," he said, placing his free hand over hers where it curled around his arm, "thanks for stepping in to help out."

"How do you know I have?" she asked, cocking her head.

"Morgan's been calling me all morning. He says you've been in the kitchen and behind the tea trolley and even changed a diaper or two, and helped with the laundry. What you've done has been noticed, and they're grateful. We all are, especially under the circumstances."

She shrugged. "It's not like I'm dying this very minute."

"Eva, you're living this very minute," he told her, squeezing her hand, "and I want you to go on living every minute. That's really all any of us can do, you know. Just live every minute we have on this earth. But you need to think about what comes next, too, Eva."

She could see that he meant it, believed it, and his conviction unsettled her, so she retreated once more to familiar territory.

"Right now," she quipped, "my stomach's doing

the thinking for me, and it thinks it's lunchtime. Let's go eat."

His shoulders slumped, but he nodded and let her lead him off to the dining room, where they enjoyed a hearty lunch and not a single moment of privacy before he went on his way again. Later, after the room emptied, Eva began straightening the buffet area. An unexpected voice at her shoulder made her jump.

"Brooks tasked me with making sure you don't overtire yourself."

She whirled to find Morgan Chatam at her elbow. He grinned at her and arched an eyebrow.

"Are you overtired, Ms. Russell?"

Striking a pose, she pressed the back of her hand to her forehead and drawled, "I am languishing, sir, languishing." He laughed. She grinned. "I'm fine. Tell your evil overlord that I even remembered to take my pills."

Morgan leaned back against the edge of the dining table and crossed his ankles, bracing his weight on the heels of his hands. "He's not evil, you know."

"I know."

"In fact, he may be the finest man I know. And that's saying something, considering he married the woman I loved."

Curious, she folded her arms. "Do tell."

Morgan smiled and bowed his head as if deciding just how much to reveal. Finally, he looked up. "I was engaged to Brigitte. Then she suddenly broke it off and married Brooks."

Eva goggled at him. "And you're still friends." It came out as much question as statement, but obviously it was true.

Nodding, Morgan said, "I was young and stupid, so it took a while for me to realize that she was ill. And that they loved each other. And me."

My wife was dying when I married her.

"He knew she was dying *before* he married her," Eva concluded.

"He did," Morgan confirmed. "They didn't want to worry me when she began having symptoms, then when they discovered the tumor and she decided against treatment, they decided not even to tell me because they knew I'd press her to grasp at any straw to save her life. Brooks had the courage, the empathy, the strength, the selflessness to let her chart her own path. He loved her more than I did. I'd have made her suffer because I wouldn't have been able to let her go when I should have. I don't think I fully understood that until I met Lyla Simone. Now I get it. I *cannot* do what *isn't* best for Lyla and Bri."

"You named your daughter for the woman you and Brooks both loved," Eva suddenly realized.

He nodded. "My wife did that."

"Wow." Eva saluted. "Honors to the missus. I think I'd be jealous." Think? She instantly and intensely *loathed* Brigitte Leland, a dead woman, because Doc Gorgeous had loved her, truly and dearly, with a once-in-a-lifetime love that was a far cry from *attraction*.

Morgan chuckled and straightened away from the table. "My wife knows how dearly she's loved, and so do I. We're very blessed."

Blessed and *prayer* seemed to be bywords in this house. Eva couldn't help thinking that even Brooks's dead wife had been blessed, even if she wasn't around any longer. It was enough to make a girl who had foresworn self-pity curl up in a ball and cry herself into the grave. Eva realized with a stab of sheer terror that she wasn't ready for that. Not yet. So, as usual, she retreated to her trusty old standby, humor.

She quipped, "Prepare to be blessed anew. By the Muffin Queen's chicken and dumplings."

Morgan chuckled and began strolling from the room. "It'll be a short-lived blessing once the hordes get wind of it."

"Suppose Jesus would forgive you for keeping it to yourself?" Eva quipped.

"He would," Morgan told her gently, "but I won't. Keep it to myself that is. I will, however, rub it in when the California contingent gets here. Dorinda adores Hilda's chicken and dumplings."

The "California contingent" came in two waves the next morning. Dorinda, the youngest Chatam sibling, and her husband, Tony Latimer, arrived with Dorinda's daughter, Melinda Leland Harris, and her family, husband JW and son Johnny, early in the morning. Dorinda's son and Melinda's brother, Reeves Leland, was on hand with his hugely pregnant wife, Anna, and ten-year-old daughter, Gilli, to greet his mother and stepfather. Redheaded Dallas—youngest sister of Asher, Phillip and Petra—put in an appearance before heading off to teach school. Brooks came, too, greeting his aunt Dorinda with an effusive hug. She actually was his aunt, having married then divorced his uncle, Thomas Leland. He introduced Eva as his transcriptionist and told the newcomers that she was currently staying at Chatam House. No one blinked an eye.

Dorinda had to be decades younger than her older sisters but at least several years older than her husband, Tony. A shapely blonde with the amber Chatam eyes and piquant cleft chin, she wore beautiful clothing. They were all, right down to six-year-old Johnny, terrified for Hypatia and, for some reason, terrified for Anna as well, whom Dorinda scolded even as she hugged her.

"Why aren't you in bed?"

"When I lie on my back, your granddaughters dance on my spinal column and paralyze my legs," Anna said. "When I lie on my side, they play soccer with my kidneys. When I sit, they try to strangle me."

"She lives in the recliner right now," Reeves said, his hand pressing against the small of her back.

"What do the doctors say?" Dorinda wanted to know.

"That I'll be lucky to make my due date in mid-March," Anna told her.

"But that's to be expected," Brooks put in. "Multiple-baby births often come early. The longer she can wait the better, of course, but the babies are a healthy size for triplets, and all the indicators are good."

"Triplets!" Eva yelped, surprised. "What's that, a Chatam trait?"

Anna sighed and laid her hand atop the huge mound of her belly. "In this case, it's a petri dish trait. We required a bit of assistance, and the process worked rather well."

"I prefer to think that we're just a pair of over-achievers," Reeves quipped, kissing his wife's cheek. "Come on. Let's get y'all into a comfortable position."

"As if," Anna muttered, allowing herself to be ushered away.

Gilli took Johnny by the hand and asked, "Wanna go up to the attic and play?"

He shrugged, and Gilli said, "The adults'll tell us if anything happens to Auntie H. Dad promised."

"Auntie H. is doing fine right now," Brooks assured them.

Thus reassured, Johnny let himself be towed off to the staircase. Eva told Dorinda and Melinda that Chester was taking their luggage up to the Master Suite and that they'd find the rest of the family in the sunroom or the family parlor. Brooks promised to return for lunch and again at the end of the workday to see his "cousins." He gave Eva a quick hug before he left, then and again after lunch, as if doing so was the most normal thing in the world. It occurred to Eva as she swallowed her pills that she'd never felt less as if she was dying. Somehow, living every minute came naturally around the Chatams.

Said "cousins," twenty-four-year-old twins, arrived in midafternoon. Lyric Latimer was as classy as her mother and even more elegant, wearing her blond hair scraped back in a neat chignon. Lyric wore an engagement ring with a diamond the size of a strawberry and carried an envelope bag the exact same shade as her shoes. In contrast, her sister Harmony looked like a walking Halloween costume and carried a guitar case.

When Eva opened the door to them, they spoke the same words in unison. "How is Aunt Hypatia?"

Eva introduced herself and told them what she knew as she led them toward the family parlor, their luggage piled behind them in the foyer for Chester to carry up to the East Suite. They hadn't gotten down the hallway before the door opened and a tall, handsome cowboy walked in with a newborn cradled in the crook of one arm. A woman and little boy crowded through the door behind him.

"Chandler!" the twins cried, startling the baby so that she threw up her tiny hands and mewed like a kitten.

"Oh, I want to see Katherine Jane," Lyric declared softly, hurrying to him on tiptoes to fold back the layers of pink blankets. "She's gorgeous!"

Suddenly Chatams spilled into the hallway from every direction, greeting newcomers of several varieties. Eva slipped into the dining room, out of the way. She felt both swept up into the warm bosom of this large, loving family and on the outside looking in. She couldn't help thinking of Ricky, and yet the person she most yearned for at that moment was not her son but Brooks Leland. That frightened her as nothing else had ever done—more than realizing she would be raising her son alone, more than having a brain tumor, more even than the thought of dying. She just wasn't sure she had the courage to love again, and if she didn't have the courage for that, where would she find the courage to live? Suddenly, dying felt like the safest thing she could possibly do, which got her to thinking about what Brooks had said about what came *after*.

She didn't sleep well that night for thinking about the possibility of an afterlife. Her aunt's version of hell wasn't something Eva wanted to contemplate, but Brooks obviously believed there was *something* on the other side of this life. He'd spoken of Heaven as a place of healing, and she wanted to believe that, but she had so many questions, and Sunday morning proved too busy to seek answers.

The Chatams literally filled the Downtown Bible Church on Sunday. Eva attended worship service simply because Brooks asked her to and everyone else seemed to take it for granted that she would. Afterward, he spent the day with the family at Chatam House, haranguing Eva to slow down, sit down or remember to take her pills. She felt self-conscious, though, hanging out with the Chatams. When she didn't sit next to him, she felt very alone in the crowd, and when she did, everyone seemed to be watching the two of them. She wanted to jump up, point both index fingers at her temples and shout, "Brain tumor, people! Hello. He's not going there a second time." Instead, she kept busy. It wasn't difficult to do with so many people in the house.

Just the babies were enough to keep her running back and forth emptying garbage cans. She didn't realize how many baby products were disposable these days. She fell into bed utterly exhausted that night, but in the morning she felt tired even after a full night's sleep.

Still, the news that Hypatia had stabilized enough for her surgery to be scheduled for the following Wednesday seemed to energize everyone, Eva included. Brooks's relief couldn't have been more obvious, and that was enough to relieve Eva.

"She's going to have a long recovery," Brooks said softly, "but compared to where we began, this is very good."

Eva felt weak with relief, as if every ounce of concern and, therefore, every ounce of strength drained right out of her.

"But she'll be okay."

Suddenly, Eva seemed to float on a cloud of relief so keen that it was almost euphoria. Almost.

"What?" Brooks asked sharply.

A strange uncertainty accompanied the euphoria, a tingling fear that all was not right…

"She's going to have a long recovery," Brooks said, keeping his voice pitched low to ensure privacy, "but compared to where we began, this is very good." He knew he shouldn't confide in Eva like this, but he couldn't share the worst of his concerns with anyone else. Oh, he was honest with the family, as honest as Hypatia would allow him to be, but he had a personal stake in this, too, and where could he take those personal concerns without alarming the family if not to Eva?

"But okay for she'll," she said, idly rubbing her head.

"What?"

She waved a hand and went back to rubbing her head. "That right?"

"Is your head hurting?" he asked, turning her by the shoulders.

"Herdin," she said.

He burrowed through her hair to find the stitches he'd put in. They looked fine, clean, dry, no swelling at all. The skin had closed and was healing nicely.

"I could take these out now, if you want," he offered.

"Tagllseelagat," she babbled.

He jerked her around. "Eva?"

Her eyes rolled like marbles in their sockets. "Slummabwidhabelda."

"Murdock!" Brooks yelled, calling for the retired doctor who had arrived with Asher and Ellie earlier. He came with his older brother, Hubner. "We've got to get Eva to the hospital."

Her knees buckled even as he spoke, but he simply dipped with her and scooped her up into his arms, folding her against his chest.

"Reddymud," she whispered into his ear.

"It's all right," he told her. "Just hang on." To Murdock he said, "My keys are in my pocket. Get the doors."

Hubner reached down for the keys, but Murdock had them in hand, along with his coat and Brooks's, which he draped over Brooks and Eva both, before they reached the front door. They flew across the porch and down the steps. He didn't want to put her down, but he couldn't get into the car with her, so he had to. She looked confused and lost when he slid into the backseat next to her. He threw his arm around her and yanked her close.

"It's okay, sweetheart. It's okay. We'll take care of this."

She tucked her face into the space beneath his chin, against the flesh of his throat. "Glibbernuck-mib," she whispered, and it sounded to him, it felt to him, like "I love you," which must have been why he wanted to weep.

"I knew she was doing too much," he said to no in particular. "I wanted to believe she was strong enough for it. I want this not to be a blasted brain tumor!" He realized he was shouting when she reached up and pressed a fingertip to his lips. He kissed that fingertip and pulled it away, whispering, "I'm sorry."

She shook her head, rubbing her face against his throat. "Bittdelig."

"It's not your fault," he told her. "It's not your fault."

She tapped his chest with her finger. "All right," he said on a chuckle, trying not to cry, "it's not my fault, either, but I'm the doctor. You're the patient, stubborn, hardheaded, beautiful patient, and you're not allowed to die. Do you understand me? You're not allowed to die."

She lifted a hand and snapped a floppy salute right into his chest. Smiling grimly, he kissed the top of her head and began to silently pray.

Please, Lord, not again. Don't ask this of me again, I beg You. Give her a chance. Please give her a chance...

Chapter Eight

"It doesn't behave like any tumor I've ever seen," Murdock agreed. "You say her recovery was even quicker this time?"

Brooks nodded. "She didn't hit her head this time or have to be sedated, and the diuretic seems to have made a difference. What made you think of it?"

"We used diuretic on an aphasic boy with seizures until we could get in and unblock his shunt." Though retired now and in his seventies, as a surgeon Murdock had performed any number of tricky procedures.

"So we could be dealing with a buildup of fluid in the brain," Brooks surmised, rubbing his chin.

"Could be," Murdock concurred. "Won't know until you get some decent pictures."

"Which she has resisted," Brooks pointed out.

"Something tells me she might be a tad more

amenable now," Murdock said, pulling open the treatment room door.

Brooks hoped that was so—and feared why it might be. He was getting in deep with her, and he couldn't pretend otherwise. If only he knew how to go forward. For all he knew, she truly was dying, and the best he had to offer her was false hope. And if she *weren't* actually dying...

God forgive him, but he almost didn't want to go there.

Gulping, he followed Murdock into the treatment suite of the emergency wing of the hospital and put on his bedside smile. Eva sat up in the bed, beaming and looking adorable.

"Hey, if I do this again, will I get three handsome doctors?"

"Two handsome doctors per patient," Murdock came back smoothly.

She threw up her hands in mock disgust. "Oh, all right, if you're going to be chintzy about it."

"And one of them has to be old enough to be your father," he added, shaking a finger.

She craned her neck, looking toward the door past Murdock. "When does he get here?"

Murdock laughed and looked to Brooks. "You have your hands full with this one."

"You think?" He pulled a stool close to the bed and sat down. "Let's get serious now."

She made a face. "I'd rather not. Serious is a brain tumor."

"Maybe not," he said. "At least not anaplastic oligodendroglioma."

"What?" She blinked at him. "But my mom…"

"It doesn't add up," Murdock told her. "The way you respond to the medications, and the medications themselves. It doesn't add up."

"Your mother was diagnosed at a time when we had fewer diagnostic tools," Brooks pointed out. "It's possible that her problem was something else, a different type of tumor or… Eva, we need to do tests."

She shook her head. "I—I can't see what that would accomplish. Whatever killed her, it's bound to be the same thing."

"Not necessarily," Brooks argued.

"What are the odds," she demanded, "that my mother, my sister and I would all die of three different types of cancer?"

"Slim," he admitted, looking her squarely in the eye.

"Ding-ding-ding-ding!" she crowed. "You win. I lose. Can't we just leave it at that? I knew going in that the game was rigged, but hey, I've had fun playing."

He bowed his head, unwilling to give in to her ridiculous sense of humor.

"At least let me see all of the records, yours and your mother's. I promise you that I won't urge you to take tests or undergo treatment that is of no real value to you."

Eva licked her lips, her mind obviously running through scenarios. "A-all right."

He breathed a sigh of relief, grasped her hand in both of his and had it halfway to his lips before he realized what he was doing. Freezing with it there, he squeezed it and let it go. "I'll fill out the paperwork, and you can sign it tomorrow. I want you resting today. Then you can come into the office tomorrow, where I can keep a better eye on you."

"Whew," she joked, "for a minute there, I was starting to feel like a kept woman."

Brooks rolled his eyes. "Yeah, like you'd ever let *that* happen. You're the hardest working sick woman I've ever known."

"Pshaw," she scoffed.

"Actually," Murdock said, "the whole family agrees that you've been a godsend at this difficult time for us. Your selflessness these last days has been widely observed and remarked on."

Eva seemed temporarily speechless, her eyes suspiciously bright. Instead of speaking, though, she finally just shook her head. Brooks wondered when the last time was that anyone expressed simple appreciation to this woman and why that was so?

He cleared his throat and pushed back from the bed, saying briskly, "Frankly, I can use your help at the office tomorrow. Things have slipped a bit lately. We can use an extra hand."

"I have two," she joked, lifting both and waving them around. "Which one would you like?"

Laughing, he shook his head.

Thank You, Lord. Thank You.

He should have known she would be more than an especially able transcriptionist, Brooks told himself, looking around the tiny office that Eva had reorganized in a flash. She'd done it almost without a thought, while tossing out quips, signing papers and answering questions. A shift here, a nudge there, a shove, a push, and the next thing Brooks knew they had twice as much space.

"Let's get rid of those stitches," he told her, shaking his head and holding out his hand.

She followed him to a treatment room and hopped up onto the table. His nurse, Ruby, assembled the tray while he pulled on gloves. Eva elected to remain sitting and bowed her head, letting her long hair flow over her shoulders. The perfume of her wafted into Brooks's nostrils, and he fought the urge to kiss the slender nape of her neck. Instead, he scolded her, mildly.

"You shampooed your hair."

"Couldn't bear it any longer."

He clipped the stitches and tugged them free, one by one, being careful not to snag the short blond hairs already growing into the shaved section.

"Does it itch?"

"Like crazy."

He took a small can out of a cabinet and blew a cooling powder over the incision site. Shaking her hair back into place, she gave a long sigh.

He chuckled. "Use a soft hairbrush for a while, and let me know if you have any drainage or lumps develop."

"Will do."

She slipped off the table and went to work. Not three hours later, he heard her in the hallway joking with a patient. An hour after that he returned a patient's chart to the reception desk and found her there answering the telephone—and moving the copying machine. Twenty minutes further on, he tracked the entire staff to the break room, where they were sharing lunch and laughing uproariously. Here, too, she'd unleashed her organizational skills. Someone had baked cookies and found a way to decorate them on the fly and arrange them to read Welcome Eva.

He walked in and picked up all three cookies with the letters of her name. Leaning a hip against the counter, he crossed his legs at the ankle and started to munch.

"Hey, boss," Ruby said, "Eva would make a good office manager, don't you think?"

He glanced around, smiled, ate his cookie and said, "She would."

"But I'm a temp," Eva demurred, looking away. "In fact, I'm as temporary as temps get."

"We'll see," Brooks told her. "Will you join me in my office after the last patient?"

"Sure."

He finished his snack, said, "Good cookies," and left them to their fun.

By the time Eva tapped on his office door at the end of the day, the rest of the staff had gone and he'd already looked through her mother's records. He'd been through hers, such as they were, with a fine-tooth comb, days earlier.

"Come in," he called.

She opened the door and stuck her head inside. "Ready to go?"

"No. Come in, sit down and listen."

Slipping into one of a pair of chairs in front of his desk, she glanced around, folded her arms, crossed her long, lovely legs and said, "Okey-dokey, let the lecture begin."

"No lecture," he said, leaning back in his chair. "A confession. I talked your former doctor into sending me your records days ago."

"Oh?"

He nodded at the computer, saying, "And there's nothing here to tell me that you have a brain tumor. He's based his diagnosis entirely on symptoms and family history. So I've gone to your mother's records, and frankly, Eva, there's nothing to tell us that she had a brain tumor, either, certainly not a cancerous one."

"What? She died! That ought to tell you something."

"Yes, but she could have died from a cyst or noncancerous tumor or an aneurysm or—"

Rocketing forward in her chair, Eva pecked the desktop with an adamant fingertip. "I was there!"

"I know that," Brooks said calmly, "and I know that she must have suffered terribly. Can you tell me about it? It's important that I know, Eva. I wouldn't ask you otherwise."

Eva took a deep breath. She obviously didn't want to talk about it, but she did. "Mom, um, complained of headaches, just headaches. Nothing too serious. Then one day out of the blue she started talking gibberish."

"Expressive aphasia. Go on."

"Aunt Donna accused her of faking, but they ran their tests and found the tumor. They gave her medicine, and it got better, but the headaches and the aphasia came back, so they tried other meds. It was a roller coaster, but eventually the headaches got worse, much worse. We didn't know if the stumbling around and blacking out was because of the tumor or the pain meds."

He was making notes and alternately scrolling through the computer data. "Looks like she was on some pretty strong stuff."

"Yes. When the convulsions started, they added

meds for that, but they thought those might be because of the chemotherapy."

"I didn't see that they did a biopsy."

"Because of where the tumor was located, they didn't think they could. The chemo was a last-ditch effort to save her life."

"And it did nothing but make her more ill," he surmised.

Eva nodded. "By the end, she was a skeleton with skin, in constant pain, unable to communicate, in horrific pain and terrified. I won't go through that."

He turned away from the computer and faced her. "I won't ask you to, Eva. You have my word on that. But we have to know what we're dealing with here. We have much better diagnostic tools now. We need to run tests." She shook her head, but he pressed her, leaning forward with his forearms on the desk blotter. "Eva, I promise you that I won't ask anything of you that I wouldn't ask of my wife."

Her gaze zipped up to his at that. "Morgan told me about her."

Brooks sat back again, unsurprised. "Did he tell you how she died?"

"Only that it was a brain tumor and that you knew she was dying before you married her."

"And that we both loved her," he guessed.

"Yes. And that you had the strength not to force her to take treatment that she didn't want."

Brooks smiled sadly. "Her options were very limited. Perhaps she would have more now, but her case was…dire. As it was, we had two good years. When she started to have vertigo, we went to a wheelchair, and that's when Morgan finally realized there was a problem. Her hearing was affected next. It was central but manifested as sensorineural."

Frowning, Eva translated that. "Uh, her hearing was affected by pressure on the central nervous system but it caused distortions like damage to the inner ear?"

He nodded. "Exactly. She couldn't tell how close the source of a sound was or always identify voices. She cupped her hands over her ears a lot."

"Got it."

"When the hearing issue became severe, sitting up made her sick to her stomach," he went on, "so she was pretty much bed-bound then, but we managed her pain without 'the hard stuff,' as she put it. Next her eyesight suffered. She lost the sight in her right eye over the course of one afternoon, but she accepted that with the same grace that she accepted all the rest."

He noticed that Eva gripped the arms of her chair so tightly that her knuckles had turned white, but he didn't stop. She needed to hear this for several reasons. She needed to understand that he knew what she could be facing, that he would never force her to endure more than she must, that she need not go through the worst alone. She needed to know that she could trust him.

"One morning soon after that I got an emergency call. It was my day off, but the patient asked for me specifically, and Brigitte insisted that we keep our lives as normal as possible. We treasured our privacy, so the nurse we'd hired to help out didn't sleep in. I called Morgan to come over and sit with Brigitte until I could get back. Then I kissed my wife goodbye, promised to return soon and left."

He leaned his head back, remembering. Morgan had come only minutes later, but it must have seemed longer to Brigitte. Perhaps she had slept, or perhaps she had lost the ability to judge time. No doubt she had been frightened because she had awakened that morning completely blind, but she hadn't wanted to tell Brooks for fear of keeping him from fulfilling his duties as a physician. When Morgan had arrived, he'd bent and kissed her forehead before announcing himself, not realizing that she couldn't see him. She'd mistaken him for Brooks and had asked him to come back to bed. When she'd realized her mistake, she'd been horrified, fearing that she'd hurt Morgan. Again. Morgan had teased her about it, suggesting they steal an ambulance and run off together. Brooks had found them there some time later, laughing about it, despite the tears that had rolled down Morgan's face, unseen by his now completely blind wife.

"What did you do?" Eva asked in a shaky voice.

What Brooks said next surprised him as much as it must have surprised Eva, for he'd never told another soul.

"I prayed with my friend, sent him home, undressed, got into bed and made love to my wife for the last time." He cleared his throat and shifted in his seat, adding, "By nightfall, her pain had outrun our ability to control it without intravenous medication, and she had made me promise not to resort to that at home." He flexed his hands, remembering. "She feared people would think I'd compromised my ethics and helped her die. So I dressed, gathered her up and took her to the hospital, where they brought her ease and she died, barely sensate, four days later."

Suddenly, Eva bent at the waist and sobbed into her hands. Shocked, Brooks shot out of his chair and around the desk.

"No!" he exclaimed, going down on his knees. "You misunderstand. I'm not saying that will happen to you. It's a whole different circumstance, except for this one thing. I'll never ask you to take any treatment I wouldn't ask of her. You can trust me not to put you through needless pain, and I won't try to make decisions for you."

"I know that!" Eva wailed, dropping her hands. "That's not why I'm crying. I'm crying because

I'm such a terrible…witch." She dropped her hands, sniffed, and muttered, "Don't you dare say I don't have an internal monitor."

Brooks sat back on his heels, hiding his smile with a bowed head, and looked up at her from beneath the crag of his brow. "What makes you say such a thing about yourself?"

"I'm jealous of a dead woman," she grumbled, wiping her eyes, "one who suffered terribly and died tragically. And was deeply loved."

Brooks didn't know what to say to that, so he said nothing.

"My husband loved me so much that he slept with a nineteen-year-old," Eva groused. "In my bed."

"Eva," Brooks soothed, reaching up to stroke her hair back from her face.

She sniffed and admitted, "I guess I didn't love him all that much, either. I loved the house and the fur coat and the convertible. I miss them a lot more than I miss him, too, and I don't really miss them at all." Brooks had to smile and shake his head. "Not that it matters," she went on. "It's too late for all that, anyway."

"Before you give up on loving and being loved, let me set up the tests," Brooks urged. "Let's figure out what's really going on inside that beautiful head of yours. If it's not good, at least we'll know for sure. Okay?"

She tapped the end of his nose with a slender fingertip. "You could talk the warts off a toad."

He chuckled and pushed up to his feet, pulling her up with him by the arm. "In that case, I'll schedule the tests. I'll also assume that you'll accompany me to prayer meeting again tomorrow evening."

She rolled her eyes. "Oh, why not?"

He laughed. "My sentiments exactly." Then he sobered, adding, "The Chatams are likely to be at the hospital in Dallas tomorrow afternoon for Hypatia's surgery. I could use the company."

She nodded glumly. "Me, too."

They strolled arm in arm to the door, but just before he shut off the light, she glanced around the room and idly commented, "This place needs rearranging."

Grinning, he spread his hands. "Do your worst. Tomorrow. It's half day."

"Right."

He could see the wheels spinning behind her harlequin eyes. They were beautiful eyes, beautiful wheels, and he could hardly wait to see what they produced. Meanwhile, he'd be praying that the tests would give them good news. He wasn't sure that he could bear anything else this time, and he seemed to be in perpetual prayer about it. Even as he helped Eva into her overcoat and traded his lab coat for his own long gray wool version, he mentally spoke to God.

Please, Lord. Oh, please. It's asking too much, perhaps, Hypatia and Eva both, but I'm asking just the same. Please. You are the Great Healer. Nothing is beyond You. I have nothing with which to bargain. All I have is already Yours. All I am that is good, You have made of me. All I can ever be that is worthwhile, I lay at Your feet. If that counts for anything, then please heal these two women, for Your glory...

And so it went until he walked into Chatam House at Eva's side to answer questions for the family about the next day's coming ordeal. It seemed only natural to stay for dinner, and to sit at the table with Eva next to him. A discussion had been raging about who should go to the hospital to wait during Hypatia's surgery, and Eva chose to voice her opinion, of course.

"You really ought to let Hilda go. She's worked her heart out for the lot of you, and she'll worry herself sick here waiting for word. She was a mess the day Hypatia collapsed."

Looks spread around the dining room, some surprised, some guilty, all understanding. A consensus quickly formed.

"You're absolutely right," Hubner said, and Murdock agreed.

"We've made enough work for her," Melinda decreed. "She needs some time off."

A play day for the children and "cousin luncheons" suddenly organized as Hypatia's siblings and their spouses claimed the right to wait at the hospital for news of the outcome of her surgery. A phone tree developed. Transportation arranged itself. Brooks noted how often Eva offered suggestions—and how often and easily they were accepted. Did no one but him realize that she essentially managed the whole thing? She didn't even bother to hide it. She meddled blatantly, but her suggestions made such sense everyone just went along without a thought. She came off as such a kook at times that no one seemed to realize they were in the presence of sheer organizational genius!

When she caught him staring at her, she made a face and demanded, "What?"

He just grinned and shook his head, wondering if she even recognized her own talents. And then he prayed that she'd have the chance to do so.

"I don't know how you do it," Brooks said, turning a circle in the newly liberated floor space inside his office.

"It's science," Eva pointed out. "You ought to understand that."

"I ought to," he muttered, "but I don't."

"Look," she said, sweeping a hand toward the desk, which now rested at an angle across the corner of the room, a computer stand behind it. "A triangle takes up less space than a rectangle because it has fewer sides. See?"

"Okay, but how did you get this bookcase to fit on this wall without covering up the light switch?" he asked, turning to the wall with the door in it.

"Easy," she explained, walking over to the bookcase on the adjacent wall. "I just shoved those shelves up against these."

"I thought of that, but it makes the end of that bookcase unusable."

"No, it creates slots for file boxes. See?" She showed him the alphabetized tabs where the files slid into place. "Then we simply transfer the reference books you use the most to the top of the file cabinets, where they're within easy reach."

The whole thing was so amazingly simple he couldn't conceive why he hadn't thought of it himself and so cunningly clever he knew he'd never have thought of it.

He put his hands to his head. "Is there a place for exploding brains?"

She reached down and picked up the molded faux leather trashcan, which made him laugh.

"I love how your mind works."

She smiled, making sweet little apples of her cheeks. "It's just common sense."

"No, it's not. It's Eva Belle brilliance." Her smile widened, and his heart tripped, so he changed the subject. "Now that you've uncovered that window by moving the bookcase, though, I'll have to buy curtains."

"Shutters," she told him. "Wood shutters with

two-inch slats, stained to match the paneling and bookcases. Easily dusted, room darkening when you need them, solid, very masculine. Like you."

He felt *very masculine* around her. He felt ten feet tall and as strong as the Mighty Men of the Old Testament—and as vulnerable as a newborn kitten. Clearing his throat, he nodded.

"I'll order them before we leave."

"Well, I guess that's everything," she said. "Still no word from the hospital?"

He shook his head. "Not about Hypatia. I don't expect to hear for some time still. About you, though..."

She groaned and plopped down on the corner of his desk. He carefully pivoted his chair.

"Your tests are scheduled for Friday morning," he told her lightly. "I thought we'd stop in and see Hypatia beforehand, if that's all right with you."

"Oh, I'd like that if you think it'll be okay."

"Sure. I thought you might be too tired to see her after the tests. We've got a full day scheduled in the lab."

Eva blinked and tilted her head. "You're going to be there during the tests?"

Yeah, he'd surprised himself with that decision, too, but he hadn't been able to convince himself just to drop her off and go about his business.

"I, uh, don't have a very heavy day." That was true, now that he'd had his appointments canceled and transferred. "I want to see the pictures as they are taken."

She clapped a hand to her chest, exclaiming, "That makes me feel so much better."

He smiled, wishing it didn't make him feel quite so happy to hear her say that. He lifted a hand to his chest, aware of a tingling there as if a limb too long immobile and deprived of blood supply now felt a rush of oxygen and life-giving blood. What she had awakened in him scared him half to death. Even if her prognosis should prove wrong, she could be afflicted with any number of life-ending or life-limiting conditions. Also, the matter of her faith, or lack of it, troubled him deeply. Plus, something more, something secretive about her told him that he knew too little and warned him not to rush in blind. Yet, he couldn't seem to stop himself.

Every day he got in a little deeper. Every day he cared a little more. One day soon it would be completely out of his hands. It was time to start praying for his own survival.

Chapter Nine

Brooks got up from the chair, asking casually, "Want to grab some dinner before prayer meeting?"

"Actually," Eva said, "dinner's on me tonight."

His eyebrows leaped. "I wasn't aware that you had the resources to—"

"I have access to a kitchen," she interrupted, "and if you'll stop by the grocery on your way to Chatam House, we'll be all set."

"By rights," he began, glancing around at his office, "I owe you more than a dinner for what you've done here this afternoon."

"And you're going to pay me," she pointed out. "Now let me do something nice for you."

Bowing his head in acquiescence, he lifted an arm toward the door. "After you."

Slipping past him, she skipped eagerly into the hall.

She wished later that she'd splurged on the

chicken breasts, but it had been so long since she hadn't squeezed every penny that Eva didn't even think before she picked up the package of chicken legs to go with the frozen spinach and noodles. The capers, onion, cream and chicken broth she appropriated from Hilda's kitchen. The single-pan dish came together and cooked up in fewer than thirty minutes, and that included skinning the chicken.

Brooks hovered around the kitchen watching while she put it all together, then they ate there, just the two of them, in that big quiet house. She sliced a tomato, just to add a little color to the plate, and when they were done, there remained nothing that couldn't be wiped up with a paper towel. Brooks sat back with a satisfied smile.

"She cooks, too," he quipped, his golden eyes crinkling at the edges.

"She has to cook if she's going to eat," Eva said. "Don't you cook?"

He shrugged. "Some people might call it that. Mostly I warm up stuff. When I'm not mooching off one Chatam or another."

"They really are family to you, aren't they?"

"Yes. Some are actual family."

"Reeves and Melinda."

"Yes. My cousins."

"You're lucky," she told him. "I don't have any cousins, and my aunt is a nightmare."

"Not lucky," he refuted gently. "Blessed."

She nodded, unsure why he suddenly looked sad.

He got to his feet. "We need to go."

The ride to the church seemed oddly strained. As they walked to the door, Brooks suddenly burst out with a comment.

"Look, it can't hurt to request prayer for a good report for your tests on Friday."

"I never said it could," she muttered, wondering what had bitten him. So much had happened in the week since they'd last been here that she'd sort of gotten used to the idea of prayer.

"The point is," Brooks went on gently, "*you* need to be the one asking."

She sent him a curious glance but said nothing to that as they had entered the foyer and others came forward to greet them.

Even without the usual presence of the Chatam triplets—only Morgan's wife, Lyla, Kaylie's husband, Stephen Gallow, Asher Chatam and his sister, Dallas and the twins, Harmony and Lyric, were in attendance—Eva felt more comfortable than she had the first time she'd attended the prayer meeting. Perhaps that was because she knew what to expect, or perhaps it was because Brooks remained at her side. Whatever the reason, when it came time for those in attendance to voice their personal prayer requests, Eva raised her hand.

"I, um, will be having some tests on Friday, and I'd reeeallly like to get good results."

Someone asked what sort of tests, and Eva quipped, "They're looking for my brain."

Even Brooks chuckled at that, but then he squeezed her hand.

Much of the prayer that night centered on Hypatia. Eva felt humbled by the personal thanks so often mentioned. The Chatam sisters must have put half the town through college and paid more light and gas bills, bankrolled more ministries, housed more vagrants, sponsored more weddings, invested in more chancy businesses, endowed more studies than all the rest of the town put together, and every time someone spoke up, someone else said, "I never knew!"

"And now you know why I love them," Brooks whispered.

"You and everyone else," Eva said, gripping his hand.

They sat quietly with heads bowed some time later while a lady several rows behind them prayed aloud for her son and daughter-in-law when Brooks's phone vibrated in his pocket. Eva felt it against her thigh. He let go of her hand to fish it out and check the message. When the lady finished, Brooks lifted his head to catch the eye of the prayer leader.

"Hypatia is out of surgery," he said softly. "It was touch and go, but she came through safely. They'll be moving her to ICU soon, and everything looks good at this point. The numbers they're showing me are strong." He sat up straight, threw his arm around Eva's shoulders and smiled broadly, relief obvious in every line of his face and body. "It's a tough recovery, but she's up to it."

A collective sigh ruffled the partition, which was quickly pushed back as the news spread through the cross-shaped sanctuary. The remainder of the meeting had a celebratory feeling to it. Everyone had questions for Brooks afterward, and he hung around to answer them, but Lyla was still in the foyer talking to Jessa Willows and her handsome husband, Garrett, who held a baby girl in the crook of his muscled arm.

"Oh, she's gorgeous!" Eva gushed. "All that black hair."

They'd named her Maggie, short for Magnolia, with the middle name of Lynn. Her ten-year-old brother Hunter couldn't keep his hands off her and kept tickling her tummy. Bri reached for Eva's hair, unbound tonight, and got her chubby fist around a long lock of it.

"Oh, my," Lyla exclaimed, trying to free Eva one-handed. Eva just laughed, but then Bri yanked Eva's head sideways and tried to cram Eva's hair into her mouth. Lyla shoved Bri into Brooks's arms and went to work opening those strong little fingers, saying, "Oh, no you don't. Let go."

"I always make an impression on the diaper set," Eva quipped as Brooks juggled the baby and

Lyla pried open a tiny hand. "It's my fault, anyway. I teased her with my ponytail last time."

Finally, Eva could gather her hair into one hand, twist it into a thick rope and tuck it into the collar of her turtleneck. Bri reached for her again, so she caught that little hand and kissed it, but Bri stubbornly reached for her hair.

"Uh-uh-uh," Brooks scolded mildly, turning away with the baby so Eva stayed out of reach. At the same time, he tried to pass Bri back to her mom. Bri wasn't having it, though. She grabbed onto his ears, "kissing" his forehead with her open mouth. Everyone laughed as she effectively mauled Brooks until Lyla managed to peel her off him.

"Baby slobber looks good on you, Brooks," Garrett teased.

"What doesn't?" Eva asked dryly.

He sent her a narrow-eyed look, drying his face with a handkerchief pulled from his coat pocket.

"Oh, all right, you're not just a pretty face," she bantered. "You're my hero."

His golden eyes narrowed further as he stuffed the handkerchief back into its pocket. "I've done nothing more than sew up your scalp."

"And take me to the Chatams and redeem my van and give me a job and set up medical tests and—"

"Stop it," he ordered quietly.

She shut up, clamping her lips together primly.

Just because he wanted her to, which was the height of stupidity. The man was a genuinely good guy, one of the best, and like every other woman in Buffalo Creek she had a bad case of the Dr. Leland Crush, but she couldn't fool herself into believing that it could ever mean anything. Even if he was right and she had a chance at a normal life—and she wasn't holding her breath on that— it didn't mean she had a chance with him.

If he ever got over his dead wife, Doc Gorgeous could have his pick of women, and after all he'd been through he certainly wouldn't choose a woman with health problems, especially if she'd lied to him from the very beginning of their acquaintance. She did her best to put all romantic thoughts of him out of her mind.

Such things usually proved quite easy. A girl with a ticking time bomb inside her head didn't waste time dwelling on the future. Eva had buried all thoughts of the future along with her personal dreams the first moment she'd realized she was speaking in a language no one else could understand, just as her mother had done before her.

No one else could understand, either, how cruel even a small taste of hope was to someone in her position. Like a drop of water to a thirsting man in a burning desert, it awakened a desperate need for more, and trying not to think about it worked about as well as trying not to breathe. Without Hypatia's surgery to worry about, Eva found herself dwelling on the upcoming tests and the *possibility* of a future. After Brooks dropped her back at Chatam House that evening, her mind spun with a hundred different scenarios of how that future might play out, and in far too many of them the handsome doc figured prominently, which wouldn't do at all.

She wanted desperately to call Ricky, but she didn't dare. For one thing, he knew nothing about any of this, and she didn't want him to. For another, just because she couldn't seem to rest was no reason for him not to sleep. Sometime during that long night, she found herself resorting to prayer. Sort of.

"Hey, You," she said to the ceiling. "If You're up there, and I guess You are because all the best people seem to think so, then I could use a little help here. We could start with a little sleep, and if it's not too much of a strain, You could do something about those tests on Friday. I'd hate for the doc to come away from that with egg on his handsome face. Can't think why else You'd take an interest, frankly, but I'd appreciate it if You did." For some reason she felt like smiling then. "Hope You've got a sense of humor. You sure gave me one. I don't know if You gave me this blip in my head or not, but I reckon You can fix it if You're of a mind to. So, good night, then."

With that, she rolled over on the comfy bed and finally drifted into slumber.

Morning came too quickly, nonetheless, but Thursday kept her busy enough that she didn't have time to worry about Friday. Brooks's partner tossed her some transcription work, and once she'd zipped through that, he asked her to take a look at the supply closet, which the practice shared. Eva's hair nearly stood on end when she got a look at that long, narrow room and its jumbled shelves. They had to be burning money on a daily basis through that one debit column.

"Who on earth is doing your ordering and dispensing?" she asked Brooks between patients.

He gave her a halfhearted shrug. "Well, our nurses are most aware of—"

"Your nurses!" she interrupted. "Your nurses are overworked already. Your nurses ought to be checking boxes on a list and handing that off to someone who tracks dollars and cents, the same someone who stocks the closet, in a logical fashion, and makes sure money gets spent where it's actually needed."

"You go, girl!" Ruby called from inside an exam room.

Brooks rolled his eyes. "Look, I have a patient waiting for me. Just take care of it. Organize it. Set up a new system or whatever. Do your thing."

Eva grinned and sauntered closer. "My *thing*, huh?"

"You know what I mean," he went on more

softly. "Just don't overdo it. Get someone to help you with the heavy lifting."

"Stop worrying about me," she whispered.

"No," he said, and then he kissed her, right there in the hallway.

It was just a peck, just a quick press of his lips against hers, and she didn't know which one of them was more shocked, she or he. He blinked, pivoted away from her and disappeared inside the examination room.

Eva stood there in the empty hallway for several seconds, her fingertips pressed to her lips, a smile growing in her heart. Then she turned and all but skipped back to the supply room.

Hypatia looked frail and tiny in the ICU bed, overwhelmed by tubes and wires and machines, but her color was good, and she was off the respirator. Best of all, she was awake and fully responsive when Brooks slid open the heavy glass door and walked into her cubicle.

"Hello, dear one," he said, walking over to kiss her forehead. "Are they taking good care of you?"

"Of course," she said in a small voice. "I'm Dr. Leland's favorite patient."

"That you are."

She felt warm, but that was to be expected after having her chest split open and her heart sliced on. He wasn't worried. Every report was positive now.

"I'm glad to see you," she told him. "I want to go home."

That set him back on his heels. "You're going to have to give it some time, dear heart. We have to get you out of ICU first. Then we'll start talking about getting you out of the hospital."

"I mean I want to go to the hospital in Buffalo Creek. I'm too far away for the family to come every day, but they won't stay away. Besides, my favorite doctor is there."

Brooks grinned. "I'll see what we can do once you're out of ICU."

"Now that that's settled," she said, as if it were a fait accompli, "is that Eva Belle Russell I see in the hallway?"

"It is," Brooks answered, motioning for Eva to come inside. "She's having tests done today. I have reason to doubt her prognosis."

Eva slid open the door and stepped inside, smiling at Hypatia. "You look so much better than I expected."

"I must look better than I feel, then," Hypatia admitted weakly.

"Oh," Eva responded sympathetically. "Can I do anything?"

Hypatia smiled, closing her eyes as if doing so required a supreme effort. "You've done so much already," Hypatia told her. "The whole family has sung your praises."

"You should see what she's done in my office,"

Brooks said to Hypatia. "The staff is campaigning to have her made office manager."

Eva shook her head, blushing a vivid shade of pink. The woman obviously had little practice accepting praise.

"I'll be praying for you today," Hypatia promised in a near whisper.

Eva nodded and blurted, "I—I prayed for you."

Hypatia smiled wearily again. "Don't stop now," she murmured, clearly drifting toward sleep.

"I won't," Eva vowed softly.

Brooks bent and whispered in Hypatia's ear, "We're all praying for you, dearest. Rest now."

He and Eva tiptoed from the room. After conferring quietly with the nurse at the station outside the window for a few moments, they left through the heavy isolation door and made their way over to the proper floor of the proper building of the sprawling, multiple city block campus. Brooks had pulled some strings and "preregistered" Eva, so all they had to do was pick up a printed, color-coded bracelet and go to a particular waiting area. Brooks identified himself and was shown through a door marked Private, where he met the radiologist who would guide and read Eva's MRI. He had requested this particular woman because of her reputation for accuracy and no-nonsense, straightforward reporting.

When the attendant asked Eva if she was claustrophobic, Eva quipped that she'd been preparing herself for a pine box, so she ought to be able to handle a metal tube. The radiologist shook her head and chortled.

"Pine box," she parroted. "Me, I'm thinking in terms of a gold-plated '57 Ford parked inside a pink marble mausoleum."

"I think in terms of Pearly Gates," Brooks said. "I couldn't care less what comes after my last breath in this world."

The radiologist, a short curvy redhead, lifted her eyebrows. "Your lady must agree with you if she's planning for a pine box. Let's see if we can buy you some time together, hmm?"

Brooks didn't bother to correct any of her assumptions. All he cared about at this moment was what the tests could show him.

It seemed to take forever, especially after the radiologist asked for contrast and they had to pump dye into Eva's veins, but with every slice of the visual, his excitement grew.

"I'm no radiologist, and I *want* to see good news," he finally said, "but that doesn't look like a tumor to me."

"That, my friend," said the other doctor, "doesn't look like any tumor I've ever seen. I'd say odds are it's a cyst, but what type I can't begin to tell you. Could be colloid. Could be dermoid. Thing looks like it could have hair."

"No way!"

"Or those could be clusters of tiny blood vessels. It might have fluid. Won't know until you get in there. Whatever it is, it's certainly a rarity in that part of the brain. One thing's for sure. It has to come out."

Convincing Eva to let a surgeon inside her head was going to be a problem. "I'm not sure she'll consent to surgery."

"Then, you'd better outfit her for that pine box," the doctor said, "because sooner or later that thing is going to blow up."

Brooks gusted a sigh and nodded. That was his prognosis, too.

"On the other hand," the spunky redhead went on, "surgery is no sure cure. It all depends on the type of cyst, the risk of infection, if it's an inheritable condition…"

"It is."

"Whether or not you can get it all…"

"I'm fully aware, thanks," Brooks said, cutting her off.

"Anyway," she went on. "Odds are better than with most tumors."

"There is that," Brooks admitted. Then he closed his eyes and thanked God. It was good news, better, anyway. He'd focus on that and keep praying. Meanwhile, he had work to do.

After what felt like a very long day, he shook the hand of the radiologist, thanked her and asked for a report to be emailed to his private account.

He'd decide later whether to show it to Eva or condense it for her. Right now, he needed to think. The idea that he could have feelings for another woman who could be knocking on death's door horrified him, especially as she did not share his faith.

Frankly, he couldn't figure out how it had happened. Eva could hardly have been more different than Brigitte. Both were tall blondes, and that's where the similarity ended. Brigitte had been a sweet, gentle soul with a slender core of steel, quintessentially feminine, with an infinite ability to love and a quiet intelligence that instinctively sought the sidelines. Eva made Brooks think of Amazonian warriors and medieval queens, strong women who buried their fears and did battle with every tool at their disposal, even if it was only humor.

Brigitte had sought to protect first Morgan and then Brooks from her illness, while preserving her own right to self-determination. He wondered suddenly whom Eva was protecting and why she had fallen into his hands. Eva had come from the Kansas City area, he knew, but why?

At first, he hadn't wanted to know. He'd assumed, hoped that she would shortly be out of his life. Now he needed to know if she was running from or to someone. What, other than the hand of God, had brought her here to this place, to him? Something told him the answer to that question was the key to both Eva's past and her future. All he could do in this moment was ask God for the courage to do and be all that he should in order to take that key in hand and open the door for her that she needed opened.

"Lord, help us both," he whispered, going out to meet her.

Chapter Ten

"Eva, I'm not a radiologist," Brooks said for perhaps the fifth time, his expression suspiciously bland. "You've got one of the best, though. She'll give us a thorough evaluation, hopefully by Monday or Tuesday. Until then we just carry on as before."

"Easy for you to say," she grumbled, reaching for the handle of the car door. "You're not faced with a long weekend of doubt."

"You could come in to the office in the morning, but I don't have anything for you to do. You took care of all of the transcription this afternoon, and you've reorganized everything but the parking lot."

She stuck out her tongue like a petulant child, and he laughed.

"That wasn't criticism," he insisted. "Tell you what, put that agile brain of yours to work on a reorganizational plan for the office as a whole, a work flow plan, personnel included. Can you do that?"

She shrugged. "I suppose. Someone needs to be ordering supplies besides your nurses."

"Okay, but who? Reception, Accounting and Records all have their hands full. That just leaves doctors, nurses and technicians."

She frowned at him. "I'll think on it."

"You do that. I'll see about getting you a tablet to work on."

"Whatever," she grumbled, opening the car door.

He waited there at the end of the brick walkway, the engine of his sedan idling, while she climbed the steps, crossed the porch and let herself into Chatam House. The great house felt oddly empty, though Magnolia appeared before Eva made it all the way across the foyer to the staircase.

"Oh, good," she said, "Maryanne and I feared we'd have to eat alone. Dorinda and Tony have gone into Dallas to spend the evening with Bayard and his family, and Odelia, Kent and Murdock are at the hospital. How did it go for you today, dear?"

Eva shrugged listlessly. "Well, they caged my head and put it in a big metal tube, then had someone pound on the tube with rubber mallets for hours. Then they pumped me full of dye and did it all over again. Then they did it with another machine. That's about it."

Magnolia chuckled. "Brooks had nothing to say afterward?"

"Yeah, he said the radiologist wants to be buried in a gold-plated car inside a pink mausoleum. Go figure."

Magnolia lifted her eyebrows. "I suppose there's no accounting for taste," she said.

Just to rag her, Eva mused, "My pine box is sounding kind of dull now. Mom used to have a shoebox covered in dyed macaroni. What do you think of that?"

"I think you'll need a lot of macaroni," Magnolia said with a straight face. "Personally, I'd rather eat it than be buried in it, but not tonight. Tonight we're having homemade turkey potpie."

"Ooh. I'm suddenly hungry."

Magnolia's mouth twitched. "We'll finish our tea and meet you in the dining room."

Eva hurried to wash up and get back downstairs.

Maryanne had come over to keep Magnolia company, while Hubner, the eldest Chatam sibling, had bowed to pressure to stay home and rest. Everyone else had returned to his or her normal life.

"I understand that Hypatia will transfer to the hospital here in Buffalo Creek once she's out of ICU," Eva mentioned over her potpie, which proved to be as delicious as everything else Hilda cooked.

The other women looked at her with surprise, and Magnolia dropped her fork. "That's wonderful!"

"You didn't know?"

"First I've heard of it." Sitting back, Magnolia pressed her linen napkin to her mouth and sighed happily.

"That will make things so much easier," Maryanne opined with obvious relief.

"That's what Brooks said," Eva told her.

"God bless that boy," Magnolia declared.

"Actually, I think it was Hypatia's idea," Eva said, "but of course, Brooks would have to arrange it."

That news lightened the mood considerably, but it didn't last, not for Eva. Maryanne rushed off right after dinner to inform her branch of the family, and Magnolia went into the library to make telephone calls to several others, leaving Eva on her own. She appropriated a notebook and several ink pens, carrying them up to her room, but she couldn't concentrate on Brooks's new office flowchart.

TV didn't help. She couldn't keep her mind on that, either. Thoughts of Ricky plagued her almost as much as thoughts of the outcome of her tests, and she missed him with a visceral sharpness that was as physical as any symptom she'd ever experienced, but she dared not call him, not yet, not unless she had reason to hope.

That was hard to do. She feared hope almost as

much as she feared the thing in her head, perhaps more. Hope raised the prospect of disappointment, and she wasn't sure she could face disappointment. Real hope could unleash the future and its myriad possibilities, one of which—dared she even think it?—could be, *might* be, some sort of personal relationship with Brooks Leland. She physically spun away from the thought, even as she yearned to latch on to it, *especially* as she yearned to latch onto it, but the idea would not stay away, no matter what she did.

Eventually she resorted to prayer again, but this time it became a rambling, angry diatribe against everything that had gone wrong in her life from the absence of her father and deaths of her mother and sister, to her ex-husband's unfaithfulness and her aunt's thousands of unkind remarks and finally to this very moment of agonizing uncertainty and the many fears that suddenly pressed in upon her. She had thought herself ready to face death. Now she wondered if the truth might be simply that she wasn't prepared to face *life*. At some point she did drop off to sleep, waking hours later from a heavy, dreamless slumber to the sound of someone knocking on her door.

She elbowed her way up groggily from her pillow and croaked out, "Yes?"

"You're wanted on the telephone, dear," said Odelia's twittering voice.

"Oh. Thank you."

Eva looked at the phone on her bedside table, wondered vaguely why she hadn't heard it ring and sat up before gingerly lifting the receiver from its base and pressing a green button. "Hello?"

"Eva? It's Lyla." An invitation to dinner followed, along with the promise that Chester would see her safely delivered to their doorstep about five o'clock that afternoon. "So we can have a good visit," Lyla said.

Eva wasted no time in accepting the invitation. Mere moments later, she hung up the phone and, relieved for something to look forward to, fell back on the bed and smiled. Abruptly, as if someone had flipped a switch, the flowchart suddenly began to churn through her mind, and she got up to jot down her thoughts before she lost them in her preparations for the day.

After a hot shower, she dressed and went down for a late breakfast, which she ate in the kitchen, while Hilda bustled around putting up lunches for those going to the hospital that day: Hubner, Magnolia, Dorinda and Tony, the twins having returned to California already. Apparently Chatams did not eat cafeteria food, but why would they if they could eat Hilda food?

The flowchart wouldn't leave Eva alone, though, and she found herself scribbling on a notepad that Hilda kept attached with a magnet to the built-in stainless steel refrigerator. Hurrying back up to her room, she wound up on the sitting area floor, notebook sheets spread out around her as she tried to make sense of the needs, duties and processes necessary to run a physician's practice smoothly.

Obviously, Brooks and his staff were overtaxed, and the partnership was farming out more and more of their work, which had to be hurting their bottom line. Patient care did not seem to have suffered; Brooks was far too conscientious of a physician to let that happen. Still, some areas of the practice approached chaos, the ordering of supplies, for instance, and the telephone system, too. Several times callers had rung through to the transcription office instead of the appointment desk, and Eva knew that the same happened with other extensions. She began to believe that Ruby had the right idea, sort of. What Brooks Leland and his partner needed was not an office manager but a manager for their *practice*.

It wouldn't be her, of course, unless...

She put away *unless* and concentrated on the reorganization, and before she knew it, the pounding in her head sent her in search of food with which to take her pills, and then it was time to get dressed and head downstairs again to find Chester. He'd already brought around the car and insisted on opening the back door for her, perhaps because she'd impulsively worn the cape. Remembering Bri's fascination with her hair, she'd coiled her long locks into a tight chignon at the nape of her neck. The overall effect did seem rather formal, though beneath the white wool and satin she wore nothing more than black leggings and a long matching T-shirt with the red heels. She'd knotted a red bandana and looped it loosely, using it almost as a necklace.

"I could drive myself, you know," she muttered to Chester, "if Brooks would give me my car keys."

Chester smiled sympathetically and said, "I think he's afraid you'd drive off into the sunset and we'd never see you again."

"I wouldn't!" she insisted indignantly. But she might have in the beginning. Besides, she owed Brooks money. He was entirely within his rights to hold on to her keys.

"I'll gladly drive you," Chester told her as she settled down into the backseat, "anywhere you want to go. If I didn't, Hilda would have my head."

For some reason, that moved Eva more than all the gratitude and compliments from the family had. She couldn't believe it, though, when Chester insisted that she keep her seat until he came around to let her out of the car after they arrived at Morgan and Lyla Simone's lovely old redbrick house.

Though not nearly as old as Chatam House, the place couldn't have been built more than twenty or thirty years past the turn of the century. It had a solid, permanent feel to it, from the red clay tile of its roof to the natural stone of its majestic chimneys, as well as a certain gracefulness in its lines and multipaned windows. The front door, with its fanciful wrought iron grille, opened as Eva slid out of the town car, but neither Morgan nor Lyla Simone greeted them from the redbrick, half-moon porch. Instead, Brooks smiled down at them.

Such delight surged through Eva that she felt almost giddy with it.

"Thanks for bringing her over, Chester," he called, "but don't worry about picking her up later. I'll bring her home."

"Very well," Chester said, winking at Eva.

Partly to hide her reaction to Brooks's presence, partly in gratitude for Chester's kindness, she kissed Chester's plump cheek. Blushing, he hurriedly shut the car door and rushed around to drop down into the driver's seat. Brooks grinned as she joined him on the porch.

"You constantly amaze," he said, looking her over, head to toe. "I don't know any other woman who can pull off that cape, but on you it works."

She bowed her head in acknowledgment of his compliment. "Thank you." Swirling the cape around her, she preceded him into the house.

The terracotta floors and light cherry wood walls of the entry hall carried through to the spacious living area and on into the sumptuous, modern kitchen. Morgan sat at a gleaming rust-colored granite breakfast bar, feeding his busy daughter while Lyla Simone stirred a large pot bubbling on the stove.

"Something smells wonderful," Eva commented.

"I hope you like gumbo," Lyla said over her shoulder.

"I'm sure I will," Eva said, glancing at Brooks, "if it tastes as good as it smells."

"It does," Morgan promised. "Lyla lived in Baton Rouge for a while, and she picked up some interesting recipes."

Lyla turned from the big black range then, brandishing a long wooden spoon. She tilted her head. "Girl, you look fine," she said, as Brooks slipped the white cape from Eva's shoulders. "Don't let my daughter anywhere near that thing, though."

"I'll just put this with my coat," Brooks said, leaving the room.

Eva parked herself on a wrought iron stool next to Morgan and made eyes at the baby, who grinned around a mouthful of carrots and rice and squished a fistful of green beans.

"Don't squeeze 'em, elf," Morgan admonished. "Eat them."

Eva picked up a green bean, squeezed it between her thumb and forefinger then calmly ate it. Bri promptly stuffed her fist into her mouth, squished green beans and all.

Morgan looked at Eva, handed off the spoon with which he'd been attempting to feed his daughter, and abandoned his stool, staying, "You seem to be better at this than I am, and I've been told to set the table."

Shrugging, Eva moved over to his stool. Brooks returned and took her former place, leaning his elbows on the countertop.

"You've been drafted, I see."

"It would seem so."

Eva waited until Bri's mouth was empty before she served up half a spoonful of brown rice with bits of juicy beef in it. Then she placed a single carrot slice in front of the baby. Bri poked at it with her fingertip then put the carrot in her mouth. After she'd chewed on all that for a while, Eva placed a green bean in front of her. Bri squished it then she ate it. When Eva offered her the next bite, she turned her head away, so Eva offered her a drink from her sippy cup instead. That was eagerly accepted, and afterward they went back to the rice and beef. In that fashion, the plate was slowly, patiently cleaned.

Eva couldn't help smiling as she fed the little one. It seemed like only yesterday that she'd done this with Ricky, like yesterday and at the same time like forever ago. Suddenly she missed him so keenly that the ache felt as physical as a cut or a broken bone. She hoped, she *prayed*, that he did not miss her like this. As badly as it hurt to think it, she hoped that he'd adjusted to her absence, that he'd settled into his new life, started to have fun with his dad, made friends with his cheesy step-mother. She wanted him to have a normal life, a good, happy life, not a life filled with grief.

Eva looked around to find the Chatams standing side by side at the end of the counter staring at her.

"What?" she asked.

Morgan pointed at his daughter. "She never eats that much for us."

Lyla folded her arms, saying, "Something tells me you've done this before."

Eva opened her mouth. To lie. But somehow she just couldn't do it, so instead she merely shrugged.

"Did your sister have children?" Brooks asked softly.

Eva shook her head. "No. Ava never had the chance to marry and start a family."

"I see. I'm sorry."

Eva nodded. "Me, too."

She told herself that maybe she could call Ricky with good news next week. Maybe she could even go home and reclaim him soon, but would he even want to see her by then?

Perhaps it would be best to leave him with his father. What then? Stay here? This was where she really wanted to be, but how could she live so far from her son?

She bit her lip and bowed her head, wondering if she should tell these good people about Ricky. No. They wouldn't understand why she'd done what she had. She'd set out to protect her son from the grief she'd experienced, and she'd hold to that, even if it meant protecting him from the good intentions of those who would call him to her side if she was too ill to prevent it. But, oh, if the news was truly good, she could tell the truth and have friends and maybe even belong somewhere. Maybe even love someone.

Oh, God, what am I doing? Eva wondered, and then she realized what she was doing. She was praying. Again. And why not? She closed her eyes and thought, *I don't want to lie to these people, and I don't want to stay away from my son. I want to live, and I want to believe. I want what these Chatams have, and I need You to show me how to get it. But that has to be Your will for me. I guess I need to start there, with Your will for me, so that's what I need You to show me now, Your will.*

Something touched the back of her hand. She jumped and looked up to find Brooks studying her.

"You okay?"

"Yes! Fine. Just…preoccupied."

He curled his fingers around hers and squeezed. "It's going to be good news, but you may have to make some decisions, and you should prepare yourself for that."

She nodded, uncertain if he knew more than he was saying or if she was reassured.

A few minutes later, Lyla put a loaf of French bread into the oven, and twenty minutes after that, they sat down to the table. Eva *did* like gumbo, but not as much as she liked Morgan and Lyla Simone. She helped clean up afterward and walked into the study with Lyla to find Brooks sprawled on the floor with Bri bouncing up and down on his chest. Eva saw the look of surprise that Lyla sent to Morgan and the smile that they shared.

As soon as Eva sat down, though, Bri climbed up into her lap and went after her bandana, which Bri obviously mistook for a teething toy. Lyla finally took her and carted her off to get ready for bed, returning some time later with the baby outfitted in ruffled pink footed pajamas.

"You're too cute," Eva told her, kissing both her round cheeks.

"And she knows it," Morgan said happily, taking her from Eva and passing her to Brooks, who now sat on the floor with his back to the sofa next to Eva's legs.

He perched Bri on his knees and bounced her up and down before kissing her in the middle of her forehead and handing her off to her mom, who settled down in the rocker right there in the room and tucked the baby tightly against her with a light blanket. Morgan lowered the lights in the room, and they all spoke in softer tones, but unlike most parents, they didn't take Bri away and put her down in a room by herself. Obviously Morgan and Lyla wanted their daughter to be a very present part of their lives, and she seemed used to it, so much so that she slipped right off to sleep in only a few minutes. Lyla kept the child with her until she grew tired of holding her, then she finally rose and carried the baby to her bed.

Morgan smiled at Eva and explained. "Lyla had cancer and had to have a hysterectomy. We feared we'd never have children, but God was preparing Bri for us all along. We can hardly bear to miss a moment with her, even when she's sleeping. Plus, we know this stage is short and we'll soon be sharing her with friends and school and the rest of the world."

Tears suddenly swam in Eva's eyes. She missed those baby years so much. She missed everything! She had to look away.

Lyla walked back into the room just then and resumed her seat in the rocker. Looking from Eva to Brooks to Morgan and back again, she carefully asked, "Were you planning to be in church tomorrow, Eva?"

Brooks leaned his head back against the seat cushion of the sofa, looking up at her. Eva cleared her throat and said, "Yes."

Lifting his head, Brooks said, "I'll take her." He leaned his head back again, explaining, "Chester and Hilda go to a different church, and I'm not sure what the aunties' plan is for tomorrow."

She smiled and nodded.

Lyla said, "We'll see you there, then. Maybe we

can make plans for later this week. Just us girls. Lunch? How does that sound?"

"I'd like that," Eva said. After she got her test results, she'd know whether it would be a celebration or an attempt to keep up her spirits.

By the time Brooks drove her home, surprisingly late, Eva felt that she'd made a true friend in Lyla. She attempted to discuss the flowchart she was drawing up for the office, but Brooks professed to be too tired to give it his attention just then and said they'd discuss it at work. Because she wasn't anywhere near to completing it, anyway, she let the matter drop and instead heard herself say, "Morgan and Lyla are really crazy about Bri, aren't they?"

"They're *insane* about that kid," Brooks retorted.

Eva grinned. "Can you blame them? She's adorable."

"To tell you the truth," he admitted sheepishly, "I'm kind of jealous."

"Of Bri?" Eva exclaimed. "She's a baby!"

"No. Of Morgan." He shot her a glance. "I'm happy that Morgan's happy. He's waited a long time for this. And I have no designs on Lyla. But he suddenly has Lyla *and Bri*, and I'm just realizing that maybe what I have had isn't enough anymore." Brooks shook his head. "All these years, what Brigitte and I had was enough, and then suddenly there was little Bri, her namesake, and somehow Brigitte is the past, and it isn't enough anymore." He shrugged. "Sounds stupid, doesn't it?"

"Not at all," Eva said. "I think everyone wants a family of their own. I always did."

"Do," he corrected. "Don't talk about yourself in the past tense. You're not dead, and you may not be dying any more than anyone else."

She nodded and let the conversation end there. They could have this conversation when the test results came in. Only one more day, hopefully, to get through before then. She thanked him for the ride home and, knowing full well that he'd engineered the dinner invitation, for a lovely evening, and went off to bed pleasantly exhausted.

To her surprise, she slept relatively well and rose the next morning glad for something with which to occupy her time. She took care dressing for church and went downstairs with the white wool cape draped over one arm.

Brooks sat at the breakfast table looking gorgeous in a black suit and pale gray shirt and tie. Sunday meals at Chatam House were, in Hilda's own words, "catch as catch can," because the staff had the day off, but Hilda had left a basket full of her scrumptious ginger rolls and a bowl of fruit. Eva "caught" two rolls, buttered them and gobbled them down with her coffee, much to Brooks's amusement.

"Laugh at me if you want," she said loftily as

he escorted her out to his car, "but those things are irresistible."

"I know," he returned smoothly. "I had four while I waited for you to come downstairs."

"Glutton," she teased.

"Guilty as charged," he admitted, grinning unrepentantly.

They bantered all the way to church, which proved to be a fresh revelation. The Chatams showed up en masse, and it was announced from the pulpit that Hypatia had been moved from ICU to a regular room. The worship service felt like a joyous celebration after that. God had never felt so real to Eva, and she prayed silently for Hypatia, Ricky, Brooks and herself during the service before listening to the sermon with sincere interest. Yet, she came away feeling somehow lacking, not quite a part of the whole. She barely had time to ponder that matter, however, as the family swept her into their dinner preparations.

With anxiety over her test results returning, Eva wasn't really hungry, but Magnolia and Odelia had arranged a kind of family potluck, and Brooks came along to make what everyone called his "famous apple tea," which turned out to be strong iced tea sweetened with organic apple juice and a touch of honey. It really tasted quite good, and just working with the family to put together the meal kept Eva too busy to ponder or worry. Only when she heard Murdock say quietly to Brooks that he'd done the research and was ready to make a recommendation on a neurosurgeon did she realize what was actually going on.

"You're all here for me," she blurted in the midst of laying the table, "because of my tests." The hubbub in the dining room immediately stilled, and all eyes turned her way. "Hypatia is out of danger now, isn't she? This isn't about her, is it?"

Brooks stepped forward. "Hypatia is doing well," he confirmed. "She will move to the hospital here tomorrow."

"We just wanted to help you keep your mind off those test results, dear," Magnolia said.

Tears filled Eva's eyes. She wanted to thank everyone, but she couldn't ignore the implications of Murdock's comment. Neither could she forget all that her mother and sister had gone through. Some of their treatments had been as bad or worse than their diseases.

"You're talking about surgery."

Brooks glanced at Murdock before slipping his arms around her. "Let's just wait for the report, sweetheart."

"You know more than you're telling me," she whispered against his shoulder.

"I told you to expect good news and that you'd have to make some decisions," he answered softly, "but let's wait for the report. All right? Just another day or so."

Eva stiffened her spine, but still she trembled

against him. "This is me expecting good news," she quipped, hanging on to him, "terrified by the possibility of good news. You should see me with bad news. I'm great with that!"

"It's all right, Eva," Brooks told her, holding her tight. "You're not alone."

And she wasn't. These people cared for her. So many people, a new feeling for her. Her mother and sister had only had her—and her bitter, hateful aunt. She felt Magnolia's gnarled hand touch her shoulder, and then another hand beside hers and another and another and another…they crowded around, quiet and caring. Eva's tears spilled over. Hubner began to speak in a raspy but authoritative voice.

"Lord, our sister Eva needs Your strength and healing…"

She had to bite her lip to keep from sobbing with bittersweet joy as their prayers flowed around her and winged heavenward.

Chapter Eleven

"I told you it was good news," Brooks said.

Perching on the corner of his desk, he watched as Eva read the printed report from the chair that she herself had rearranged during her organizational spree, her pale head bent over the file folder. He had prayed much and discussed seriously with Murdock about whether to let her see the full report or to present her with a condensed, best scenario version. With any other patient, he'd have presented an oral report and made a firm recommendation, but Eva was different. For one thing, her understanding of medical issues superseded that of most patients. For another, he was more than half in love with her. And he had been down this road before. He had never sugarcoated anything for Brigitte, and he couldn't bring himself to do it for Eva. He had to be honest with her and hope she'd give herself, them, a chance.

It had been an eventful day filled with patients,

seeing Hypatia settled into her room at the hospital across the street. And now this. The report had come in just after lunch, but he'd kept it until the end of the day so they could have privacy and time in which to discuss it.

"A cyst," she finally said, placing the open file on the desk. "And you think a cyst like this may have killed my mother."

"It's possible. We can't know for sure. We won't even know exactly what we're dealing with in this case until we get in there and see what kind of cyst it is."

Eva sat back and crossed her arms. "They told Mom that her tumor, cyst, whatever, was inoperable."

"It likely was. *Then.* Or hers may have been positioned differently. It's impossible to tell at this point. Yours, though, *is* accessible. We need to remove it, biopsy it just to be thorough, and go from there."

"Why not just biopsy it first?"

"There's no point in that. We need to excise the mass. We can biopsy the tissue just to be sure we know what we're dealing with, but if it's a cyst of the type we suspect, and chances are very high that it is, it has to come out. Medication alone won't take care of it."

"This report says that there's an eighty percent possibility of getting it all," she pointed out.

"If we don't get it all, we can kill the remaining tissue with radiation and medication. If we find cancer, which I do not expect, we can think about chemo, but the chances of that are very, very slim."

"And if I go through all this, you don't get it all, and it is cancer?" she asked.

All he could do was repeat what he'd already said. "In my opinion, the chances of it being cancer are very, very slim."

"And if I don't do it?"

"You're going to die. Could be a year. Could be months. Could be weeks. I can't predict how soon but far sooner than you should."

She nodded, reached out and closed the file. "I'll get back to you."

He came up off the corner of the desk. "Get back to me? Eva, we need to schedule this surgery ASAP."

She leaped to her feet, both forefingers going to her temples. "You're talking about opening my skull and cutting into my brain! I read the report. There are no guarantees. Even if the surgery is successful, I could have brain damage. I need to think about this."

"Fine," he snapped. "You think about it. Just try not to die while you're at it!" With that he turned and walked out of his own office.

He'd known she was going to be difficult about this! Why had he let himself care so much? How did he stop now? Didn't she realize that without this she had no chance, *they* had no chance? Would she really ask him to love another dying woman? Would God really ask him to love another dying woman? He couldn't do it. He wouldn't do it.

"It's all good news," Magnolia said, sitting back with a sigh and lifting her teacup. She sipped delicately and smiled at an unusually glum Eva. Apparently things were not going well between Eva and Brooks; that or they were going too well for the good doctor's comfort. "Hypatia is improving every day," Magnolia went on. "It's painful, I'm sure, but she never complains and insists that she'll be home in record time."

"I don't doubt it," Eva told her, "but this was only her fourth day out of ICU, and I suspect Brooks will want her to stay in the hospital at least until the end of the week."

"We'll let him fight that battle," Magnolia advised sagely. "Whenever she comes home, we will be prepared, though, and I appreciate your help with that, dear."

"Oh, I haven't done anything. Brooks told me to make a list of private therapists for you to interview, and that was all I did."

"Ah," Magnolia said, sipping her tea.

"Actually," Eva went on after a moment, her tone bright, "Brooks hasn't spoken a word to me in over twenty-four hours, not since he dropped me off after work on Monday."

"Hmm," Magnolia hummed. She'd known that Brooks had asked Chester to drive Eva to and from work today. Apparently he was not happy with his transcriptionist just now, and Eva's overly jolly announcement proclaimed her culpability in the matter. Interesting. "Well, I'm sure he's just busy."

"I'm sure he's mad as a wet hen," Eva muttered, but Magnolia pretended not to hear her.

"You suggested the hospital bed, the recliner and the bath seat," Magnolia said. "That was very helpful."

"It's just basic protocol," Eva protested, shaking her head, but Magnolia waved away her self-deprecation.

"Perhaps, but none of us would have thought of those things. It's been a long time since we've dealt with an invalid in this household, and we didn't have access to all these amenities back then. Kent has ordered everything you suggested, and Chester and I will interview the therapists on the list you've compiled. We've already hired a nurse recommended by our niece Kaylie, so we'll be fully prepared whenever Hypatia arrives."

"That's good," Eva warbled, her voice not quite as bright as before. "Can't have Silk-and-Pearls languishing in a flat bed and taking sponge baths for weeks on end."

Magnolia chuckled. "No, indeed. Now," she

said, setting aside her teacup, "would you like to tell me what's bothering you?"

Eva shot her a surprised glance then put on her old, cheeky demeanor. "Hmm, let me think." She tapped her chin with a slender forefinger. "Oh, yeah. I've got this time bomb ticking inside my head."

Magnolia folded her hands, regarding the younger woman shrewdly. "I notice that you no longer call it a tumor."

Eva sighed. "I don't know what it is. No one does."

"What does Brooks say?" Magnolia wanted to know.

"He thinks it's a cyst."

"But you don't agree?"

Eva merely stared into her cup for several seconds, then she shrugged. "I don't know. I only know that my mother tried every treatment the doctors offered her, and she suffered terribly. And then she died anyway." She turned an agony-filled gaze on Magnolia. "It was the same for my sister. They cut on her and cut on her and cut on her. Every time they thought they got it all, and every time, the cancer returned. Her cancer was so aggressive that her doctors encouraged me to have radical mastectomies even though I had no signs of malignancy."

"Oh, Eva, I'm sorry," Magnolia said with all sincerity. What horrors this child had seen. It broke Magnolia's heart. "I didn't realize. But, dear, don't you see that God has already protected you from your sister's disease?"

"But why didn't he protect her?" Eva demanded. "Why couldn't He save Ava?"

"I can't answer that," Magnolia replied honestly. "Did you ask Him to? Did she?"

Eva shook her head. "Not really. No."

"Don't you see that with the advances in science that God has given us and your growing faith, this could all be very different for you?" Magnolia asked.

"But what if the doctors are wrong?" Eva whispered.

"What if they aren't?" Magnolia returned. "Ask yourself this, dear. Do you really think Brooks would steer you wrong?"

Eva frowned. "I'm not Brigitte."

"Does that mean you think you're just another patient to Brooks?" Magnolia asked. "Or that he would do less for one than another?"

Turning up her hands, Eva shrugged at the same time that she shook her head.

Magnolia made a sound of frustration. "Eva Belle Russell! There's no such thing as just another patient to Brooks Leland, and even if there was, you wouldn't be one of them."

"No?" Eva asked hopefully.

Exasperated, Magnolia rolled her eyes. "No. Now, you listen to me. I don't know what God's plans are for you, but I cannot believe He would bring you into Brooks's life only to let you die. I don't believe that for a minute. But you've got to grasp what He's given you, young lady. I know you've found some faith by this time. Put it to use!"

"Yes, ma'am," Eva said, smiling shakily and blinking back tears.

"Now give me your hand," Magnolia commanded. Eva reached out with her hand. Magnolia clasped it, bowed her head and started praying.

Honestly! She'd warned this child what she'd do if she dared to hurt their dear Brooks, and she meant it, but Eva had made some significant strides. Magnolia had hopes for the girl, high hopes. She saw the way Brooks looked at her, the way he cared for her. They all did. Now Eva needed to see it. Magnolia beseeched her God to give Eva the courage needed to do what must be done and Brooks the patience and wisdom to help her do it.

Afterward, Eva seemed to be biting her lip to keep from laughing, even as her tears flowed. She hugged Magnolia, then she excused herself to make a phone call. Magnolia suspected that Brooks would be speaking to Eva again very shortly.

Eva went straight upstairs and used the house phone to call Brooks and tell him to schedule the surgery. Despite his obvious relief, he didn't waste time chatting about her decision.

"Thank God," he exclaimed. Then he got off the phone with her so he could call the neurosurgeon whom Murdock had recommended, promising to have details for her the next day.

Now that the decision had been made, Eva felt lighter of spirit than she had in some time. Determined not to worry about failure, she went to a drawer in the dresser and dug out the unregistered mobile phone she'd bought when she'd left Kansas City. Every day she fought the urge to check on her son. He had no way of reaching her because whenever she called him from this phone, the number was blocked on his end, but maybe that would soon change.

She carried the tiny phone to the sofa and sank down into its corner. Kicking off her shoes, she pulled up her feet and tucked them beneath her before whispering a quick prayer and dialing the number of her ex-husband's home.

The phone rang three times before Ricky answered with a desultory, "Yeah?"

Strangely, he always seemed to answer when she called.

"Hey," she replied chummily. "How you doing, big guy?"

"Mom!" he gasped. "Where are you?"

She hesitated a moment before answering him with a partial truth. "Texas."

"What are you doin' down there?"

"It's a long story, son, but I've found a real nice place here, and—"

"Well, good for you!" he all but snarled. "And I'm stuck here with Dad and Tiffany. That's so lame, Mom! They don't want me, especially *Tiffy*. Ugh. I'm so sick of her and the way Dad takes up for her. 'She's young. She doesn't mean it. She's never had a kid before,'" he mimicked. "Well, I'm ten. Okay? And it's not my fault she got between you and Dad. All she cares about is shopping, and all he does is work to pay for her stuff. Honestly, neither of them wants me here. I can't—"

"Ricky," Eva interrupted, "I'm trying to tell you that if everything goes as I hope, I can bring you down here with me in a few months."

"Months!" he erupted. "Don't you get it? I'm dying here!"

"You're not dying," she scoffed. *I am dying,* she thought. Except, she wasn't dying. Maybe. If Brooks was right. And of course Brooks was right. He was Brooks, after all. It hit her, finally. She was *not* dying. She didn't *have* to die. A giddy elation filled her. She barely heard what Ricky was saying.

"…hardly ever home, and when they are, she wants me to stay in my room. She says they can't be themselves with me around and I shouldn't see what they do. She's probably right, 'cause they drink all the time, and no matter what I say, I'm sassing. It's not fair!"

"Son," Eva said, forcing herself back to the conversation, "it's going to be okay."

"Come get me," he demanded. "Right *now.*"

"I can't do that," she told him. "Just give me time to…get on top of some things here. Then I'll come. I promise. And I'll explain everything."

"You don't want me, either," he accused.

"I do, Ricky," she vowed, sitting up straight, "so much, more than you can possibly imagine. Obviously I—I made the wrong choice for you. I thought a two-parent family would be best for you."

"Ha!" Ricky said. "A no-parent family is more like it."

"Okay," Eva told him. "I get it, and I'll fix it, but you have to give me a little time."

"I can't take much more of this, Mom," he warned.

"Just a little more time," she urged, "then I'll explain everything, and we'll start a whole new life together."

"You left me," he accused, his voice trembling.

"I know, and I'm sorry," she apologized softly. Maybe, she decided, the time had come to act in faith. She'd agreed to the surgery. Now she had to act as if the surgery would be successful. "I'm going to give you a phone number," she said, "for this place where I'm staying. I have friends here, good friends, and they'll know how to reach me if you need me. Okay? And as soon as I can come for you, I will. I promise."

"You better," he grumbled, and she could hear him scrambling around for something to take down the number.

"Ready?"

"Go ahead."

Somebody shouted that his dinner was getting cold, so as soon as she'd given him the ten digits, Eva told him they'd better ring off.

"I'll call again in a few days," she promised. "Say hello to Donita for me. Love you."

He grumbled, and he didn't return the sentiment before he hung up, but she was glad that she'd called. This conversation had confirmed for her that she was doing the right thing. Rick and Tiffany were never going to step up and be the parents that Ricky needed them to be. She had to do all she could in order to be there for her son.

Whatever else came after her surgery, she was going to get well and be a mother to her son, a better mother than she'd been to date. When she did finally leave this world for the next, she intended to make sure that her son had the opportunity to join her there, something she'd never considered before she'd met these Chatams and their friends. Aunt Donna's Christianity had been all about hell; the Chatams' Christianity was much more about Heaven. What mother didn't want that for her child?

For the first time in months, years, really, Eva realized that she was looking to the future, not just existing day-to-day, moment-to-moment. From the day her marriage had fallen to shreds around her and she and Ricky had been left to fend for themselves, she had been treading water, just holding life and limb together, until her symptoms had shown up, at which point she'd simply let go. She'd surrendered her son, her precious boy, to her selfish, self-centered, almost continually absent husband and his equally self-absorbed second wife—and run, accepting death like the coward she was. How had she convinced herself that it was best for Ricky?

"God forgive me," she said aloud.

She should be fighting for her boy, fighting for her life because Ricky needed her, because he needed to see her fighting for him, and they hadn't a moment to lose. In fact, she could only pray that it wasn't too late.

"One week from today," Eva echoed, looking at Brooks across the expanse of his desk.

"I know it seems quick," Brooks said, leaning forward and picking up the ink pen on the blotter, "but I'd have it scheduled for today if it was up to me. Unfortunately, the better surgeons have heavy schedules, and a week is pretty amazing, all things considered."

"I'd like it to be sooner, too," she said, surprising him.

"Oh." He sat back, clicked the pen and tossed it onto the blotter again. "I'm glad you feel that way because we have a consultation with him this afternoon."

She tilted her head. "We?"

His heart *thunked* against the wall of his chest. All right, so he'd overstepped, but he had no intention of letting her walk into that appointment alone. For one thing, he didn't trust her not to change her mind. For another, he didn't want to wait to hear what the surgeon had to say after reviewing the radiology report. The third reason was the one he gave her, though.

"I don't think you should be driving alone."

She nodded slowly. "I see."

For some perverse reason, Brooks heard himself say, "But if you prefer, I can ask Chester to take you to the appointment. He certainly knows the way to the hospital up in Dallas. He's made the drive enough times at this point."

She just sat there staring at him for several long seconds before she shook her head, rippling that lovely pale hair. "I wouldn't want to put him out unnecessarily. Besides, I'd like you to be there. You're my doctor."

He pivoted his chair to the computer, hiding

both his relief and his disappointment, and remarked dismissively, "We'll leave at two o'clock, then."

"All right." She rose and smoothly left the room.

Brooks braced his elbows on the corner of the computer desk and dropped his head into his hands. He didn't know what he was doing anymore. He hadn't even thought before he'd made that appointment and cleared his afternoon. He'd just *assumed* that he would be going with Eva, the way he'd always accompanied Brigitte to her appointments with all the specialists they'd consulted. The idea that she hadn't expected him to go, hadn't wanted him to go, had hurt, and that was foolish, idiotic. That she might want him to go only to provide transportation and because he was her doctor was equally painful and that was equally stupid on his part.

Leaning back in his chair, he looked up at the ceiling. *Of all the women in the world*, he silently asked, *why her?* But no answer came. Instead, Ruby tapped on the door and stuck her head into the room, saying, "Three patients ready and waiting."

Nodding, he got up and went to work. Answers—and Eva Belle Russell—could wait. Until 2:00 p.m.

Surprisingly, two o'clock came quickly, almost before Brooks knew it. With one patient lined up after another, he barely had time to think, let alone brood. He didn't even have time for lunch, and Eva had noticed. As soon as they got in the car, she handed him a warm, cheesy, grilled chicken wrap loaded with shredded lettuce and sliced tomato, along with a cup of hot broth and a bag of almonds.

He peeled the paper off the microwaved tortilla wrap and smiled at her. "Thanks."

He bit off the end of the sandwich, then took two more big bites, finishing the wrap before putting the transmission in gear. She just smiled and passed him a paper napkin.

By the time they reached the highway, the broth was cool enough to drink. He saved the almonds until they were walking from the parking garage to the appropriate hospital tower, finishing them just before they reached the surgeon's office. Dusting his hands, he stuffed the empty bag into his coat pocket and escorted her inside.

The tiny waiting area was empty, but a receptionist opened a glass partition and welcomed them by name, asking them to come straight through. Brooks opened the door beside the reception counter and held it for Eva. They found themselves in a quiet, spacious, luxurious area filled with attractive desks, chin-high partitions and healthy plants. An attractive woman in a business suit took them to a cubicle where they answered a few questions while she typed into computer, then she walked them through to a idiculously large examination room.

Brooks hung their overcoats on hooks beside he door before looking around. "I obviously :hose the wrong specialty."

Eva narrowed her eyes at him. "You love what rou do."

He chuckled. "True. But I *can* wish it paid bet- er."

"You could get a handle on all the cash the prac- ice is bleeding," she said dryly.

"I thought that's what you were going to do," ιe told her.

She sent him a narrow-eyed look. "Hey, I'm vorking on it. I've been just a little distracted."

He chuckled. "Uh-huh, and what's going to be rour excuse when the intruder inside your head s gone?"

Before she could retort, the door opened and he doctor walked in. An older man, surprisingly arge and not at all neat in appearance, he stood n stark contrast to his surroundings. His thin- ιing hair stuck up in odd places, his glasses were ;mudged and his clothing rumpled. Eva looked o Brooks with something very like shock in her nottled-green eyes. He gave her an almost imper- :eptible shrug and stuck out his hand.

"Sir," he said, more for her benefit than any- hing else, "you come very highly recommended."

"I should hope so," the fellow chortled, pinning

Eva with his gaze. "Is this the case, er, patient?"
He shook Brooks's hand then, but the gesture wa
clearly an afterthought.

"Uh, yes. Eva Russell."

"Interesting," he murmured, peering at he
skull as if he could see inside her head. Abruptly
he waved a hand. "Sit, sit." Then, without wait
ing for either of them, he plopped himself dow
on a rolling stool. "I have no bedside manner to
speak of," he admitted forthrightly, "but I'm a bet
ter than average mechanic, if I do say so myself
much better than average, frankly. You'd know
that, though, or you wouldn't be here. Now, let'
take a look."

He rolled himself over to the light viewer an
flipped it on. The pictures were already mounted
Brooks handed Eva down into a chair and pulle
one forward for himself. The fellow ran an effi
cient operation, Brooks would give him that much
Over the next ten minutes, he convinced Brook
that he had a lot more going for him than that
After he had thoroughly impressed Brooks, he
picked up a folder and handed it to Eva.

"Personalized pre and postsurgery instructions
Postsurgery instructions are divided by best and
worst case scenarios. I'll let you know on the day
of surgery and again when you're released from
the hospital which set you are to follow, and I ex
pect you to follow them to the letter." He waved
a hand at Brooks then and said, "But he'll know

hat's best, in any event. Lawyers make me say at other. Make our job a pain sometimes, lawers, don't they?"

"I guess they can," Brooks answered diplomatically.

"Spoken like a man who's never been sued," he other doctor grunted.

"Well, no, I haven't," Brooks said.

"Me, neither," the neurosurgeon announced roudly. He grinned. It was not a particularly leasant sight. "Shocked you, haven't I?"

Brooks laughed. "A little bit."

The surgeon turned his sights on Eva. "Got any uestions before I call it a day?"

"Recovery time," she answered immediately.

"Depends," he told her. "Could be a week. ould be six months."

"Six months!" she yelped. "I have to be able to avel before that!"

Brooks's head whipped around. Travel?

"Out of my hands," the surgeon was saying. If all goes as I expect, a month or so, but I said , and I mean *if.* There's no way of telling until get in there, and then I can't make any guaranes. You know the risks, everything from bleeds infections and stroke."

Frowning, she muttered, "A month. And that's est case." Her shoulders slumped, and for a moent she looked so woebegone that Brooks curbed e urge to slip his arm about her.

Just where was she planning to travel? On
thing was certain, she wasn't planning to trave
anywhere *with* him so she could only be plannin
to travel *away from* him.

Well, what had he expected? She'd been goin
somewhere when she'd tumbled into his life. Wh;
made him think she wouldn't resume the journe
as soon as she was able? He wished suddenly tha
he'd never redeemed her van, then recalled tha
he'd done it just so she would move on. The iron
of that made him want to slap himself. Only a
they walked back to the car did he realize tha
she knew nothing of his feelings for her, but ho
could she when he was just beginning to unde
stand them himself?

Chapter Twelve

Hope. Eva had thought of it as a nasty four-letter word, one that could only bring her and her son pain, until she'd actually caught a case of it. Now that she had hope, it felt grand, and she wasn't about to give it up again. That was why she asked Brooks to take her to prayer meeting again that evening and why she freely requested prayer for a good outcome to her surgery. People seemed to recognize the fact that she was having surgery at all was good news, and she felt comfortable telling a cluster of ladies afterward that she really needed to get on her feet and functional as quickly as possible.

"Places to go and people to see," one of them bantered.

"Exactly! I have a life." She wiped a hand across her brow. "Whew."

Everyone laughed, not realizing just how completely she meant that statement. She noticed that

Brooks frowned when he heard it, but he didn't say anything about it later on the way back to Chatam House. Instead he talked of the fact that Hypatia would be returning home in just two days, on Friday, and whether the household had been adequately prepared for her. Eva felt sure they were ready, and he seemed to accept her assurance on the matter, which she found gratifying.

Over lunch on Thursday she finally shared her story—the medical part of it, anyway—with the girls in the office, and during the afternoon break they gave her a list of Bible verses dealing specifically with hope, advising her to memorize them, one at a time. While waiting for Brooks to finish his last appointment of the day, she started working on the shortest one, Romans 12:12, repeating it over and over to herself.

"Be joyful in hope, patient in affliction, faithful in prayer. Be joyful in hope, patient in affliction, faithful in prayer..."

Once sure that she had it down, she moved on to Psalm 33:22. "May Your unfailing love be with us, Lord, even as we put our hope in You. May Your—"

Before she got through it the second time, the phone on her desk rang. Expecting it to be another switchboard mistake—they happened often at the end of the day—she answered ubiquitously.

"Medical office."

"Eva?"

She sat stunned for several seconds. "R-Rick? How did you get this number?"

"I called the one you left with *your* son," her ex answered smartly, "and someone there gave this one to me."

She gripped the edge of her desk. "Has something happened to Ricky?"

"I wouldn't know," he snapped. "The little snot took off."

"What?" She shot to her feet. "Where did he go?"

"I have no idea."

He had no idea where their ten-year-old son had gone, and the very tenor of his voice told her that he had no intention of even looking for him!

"Who have you called, Rick?" she demanded.

"I called *you*, because you created this mess, so *you* are the one who is going to deal with it."

"You were fine with it. You wanted him to stay with you."

"That was before I knew what a demanding little brat he's turned into. He's pulled his last stunt with me, Eva. I'm done! You get back here and do something with him. I mean it. I've had it."

"When did he leave?" she asked frantically.

"I don't know. Sometime last night, I guess."

"You *guess*?"

"I can't watch him every moment."

"Or *at all* apparently! What do the police say?"

For the first time, he sounded somewhat abashed. "I, uh, haven't called them."

"You haven't even called the police?" she practically screamed. "He's been gone for *hours*!"

"I thought he'd give up and come home by now," he admitted grudgingly.

"Call them *now*!" she demanded, grabbing her handbag from a drawer and moving around her desk. "Then start calling his friends."

"I don't know any of his friends. As far as I can tell, he doesn't have any."

"Of course, he—" She broke off. What was the point? "I'm on my way, but I'm at least nine hours from you, so call the police *now*, or so help me, Rick, when I get there—"

"All right, all right," he growled. "Just get up here because he's not staying."

"No, he's not," she agreed, her anger giving way to panic. She broke the connection and tossed the phone at the desk, crying, "I was crazy to think he'd be okay with you." Then she ran down the hall toward Brooks's office.

He stepped out of an examination room just as she passed it, and she whirled to face him, dashing tears from her eyes with one hand. "Eva, what on earth is going on?" he asked. "I heard you shouting all the way down the hall."

"I need my keys."

He stepped up and ran his hands down her arms

as she nervously shifted from foot to foot. "Sweetheart, what's wrong?"

"Brooks, I have to leave. I need the keys to my van. I've worked off the debt, haven't I? It's been weeks. Please. I have to go. Now!"

Taking her by the arm, he turned her and walked her swiftly into his office. "What's going on?"

She shook her head, trembling head to toe. "There's no time. I have to get back to Kansas City. I have to find…"

"Eva," he urged, sliding his hands across her shoulder blades, "tell me. Whatever it is, I'll help you."

She gulped down the lump in her throat and wailed, "I have to find my son!"

Brooks reeled back, his eyes wide. "Son," he parroted.

"He's ten years old," she sobbed, caving in on herself, "and I didn't want him to watch me die the way I had to watch my mom, so I left him with his lousy father and went off on my own. I abandoned him!"

"You have a son," Brooks said, as if she hadn't been telling him that.

"He ran away sometime last night," she howled, "and his rotten father didn't even notice until sometime today. He says he won't look for him and he won't keep him any longer. He didn't even call the police until I threatened him!"

Brooks frowned. "Well, then we have to go get him."

"That's what I'm trying to tell you!" she yelled, stomping her foot and sticking out her hand. "So cancel the surgery and give me my keys."

"No," he said calmly, sliding an arm around her and turning her toward the door, "and no."

"What?" she asked, stumbling forward.

"I said, no, we're not canceling the surgery and no, you cannot have the keys to your van."

As he had all but shoved her through the door to his office at this point, she found herself standing in the hallway. "Brooks," she pleaded, turning her head to look up at him, "you don't understand. I have to go after my son."

"You don't understand," he told her, walking her bodily toward the coat cubby. "I'm not letting you go alone." Before she could fully digest that, he called out to his nurse. "Ruby! Bring me the new travel bag in the supply room."

"Sure, boss."

He pulled Eva's coat from the hanger and bundled her into it then he reached for his own. Ruby arrived on the scene while he was buttoning up.

"Here you go."

"Thank you. We're leaving," he said, tucking the thick, flat square bag under his arm.

"Oh. Okay." Clearly surprised, Ruby asked, "How long will you be gone?"

"I don't know," he answered. "Shift or cancel

everything you can for tomorrow and Saturday. I'll call Murdock and Maryann Chatam from the car and ask if they can come up and cover me for next week. I've already blocked out Wednesday and Thursday, so it shouldn't be too much of an issue. Beyond that, we'll see."

"A-all right. Whatever you say."

"I'll keep you posted," he promised, sliding an arm around Eva's shoulders and calmly walking her toward the exit. "If you have questions, call me."

"Will do," Ruby said.

"I don't know what to say," Eva told him in a fractured voice as they stepped out into gray winter twilight and the door closed behind them.

"Then, don't say anything." He paused to gently turn up her face with a finger curled beneath her chin. Then he kissed her, his lips descending to press softly against hers.

Eva grabbed handfuls of his coat and hung on, pushing herself up into that kiss with everything that was in her heart, taking strength and hope and warmth from it. He wrapped one strong arm about her, anchoring her firmly to this world, to him, to the hope and faith he'd brought into it.

When he lifted his head, she tucked her face into the curve of his throat and whispered against his skin, "Brooks. Brooks."

The verses she'd memorized earlier ran through her mind.

Be joyful in hope, patient in affliction, faithfu
in prayer...May Your unfailing love be with us
Lord, even as we put our hope in You.

She had hope, such hope, and she would do her
best to be patient, knowing that she wasn't alone
Never again would she believe herself to be alone
Even when Brooks Leland became a fond memory
from her past, she would not be alone.

"We'd better pack a couple of bags," Brooks
said, urging her forward.

They moved off swiftly, Eva feeling that she
saw things clearly for the first time since her original diagnosis, perhaps for the first time ever.

Hope, she thought, was a beautiful thing. She
would be foolish, though, to hope that she and
Brooks could truly have more than friendship
something permanent and blessed by God. He
loved a woman who had died long ago from a
condition very similar to hers, a woman he hadn'
been able to cure. It was natural that he would
seek to fulfill that old dream through Eva and
that he would transfer some of those old feelings
to her in the process, but she couldn't expect those
feelings to endure. In some ways, she felt as it
she was taking advantage of Brooks, but for her
son she would do what she must and try to make
amends later.

Ricky needed her. She had to find him, and if
possible, she had to stay alive. For him. She would
think of Brooks later and herself not at all. That's

what she should have done from the beginning, but until she'd met Dr. Brooks Leland and the Chatams, she hadn't even known how. As they sped toward Chatam House, she silently thanked God for stranding her in Buffalo Creek, Texas, and placing her in the care of the best-looking doctor in town and his trusting, praying friends.

She grabbed her clothes and the burner phone, explained everything to Magnolia, who promised to pray, and was waiting impatiently on the porch of Chatam House when Brooks returned seventeen-and-a-half minutes after he'd dropped her off, having changed his clothes, packed a bag and gassed up the car. As they drove north, Eva called Rick's house and spoke to the housekeeper, Donita, who basically confirmed everything Ricky had told his mom and gave her the names and contact information of his friends. Next, she called Rick's personal cell and made certain that he had spoken to the police, and then she called the police and spoke to the officer with whom Rick had filed the missing person's report on their son. She relayed to him the names and contact information of Ricky's friends and, when pressed for an address where she would be staying in the city, gave her Aunt Donna's. Donna was her next call. Eva kept it brief, knowing that Ricky wouldn't go to his great-aunt and that her own welcome would be none too warm. After that, she phoned every one of Ricky's friends to ask if they'd seen him.

Each boy denied having seen or spoken to Ricky in at least a day. Some said it had been several days or even weeks since they'd had contact with him. A couple of the boys admitted that he'd talked about running away from his dad's house, but none confessed to helping him. One mentioned another boy, Jared, but Eva didn't know him, and neither did the boy who mentioned him. After that, all Eva could do was pray.

Brooks made his phone calls, too, and received several before the hour grew late. They made good time, listening to music and talking, mostly about Ricky. It helped Eva to talk about her boy. His dad had left them when he was only five, so for half of Ricky's life, Rick had been a two-weekends-a-month dad.

"All fun and games," Brooks guessed.

"Exactly," Eva said. "He didn't even pay his child support half the time, so while I was being the world's best medical transcriptionist to keep us housed and fed, he was playing paintball, seeing matinees of all the best kid movies and keeping his new young wife happy. Tiffany never came along on visitation with Ricky and his dad, and I stupidly thought she was being thoughtful," Eva went on, "but now I realize that I gave her too much credit. She just didn't want anything to do with Ricky. I thought we were both giving them 'guy time,' because a boy needs his dad."

"Mmm-hmm, but it's not his dad who Ricky wants to live with, is it?" Brooks pointed out.

Eva smiled even as tears gathered in her eyes. Again. "Score one for the world's best medical transcriptionist," she quipped.

"Oh, I think the score is a lot higher than that," Brooks drawled.

"I sure can't claim to be the world's best mom," she admitted morosely. "What was I thinking?"

"You were thinking that you didn't want him to carry the same pain through life that you have carried."

"Yeah. I was thinking about me and my pain, and I just gave up."

"We only know what we know at any given time, Eva," he told her. "You know better now."

"All I care about right now is finding him," she whispered.

"We will," he promised. "The world's best medical transcriptionist's son can't be stupid. He'll have a plan. He'll be safe somewhere, and wherever that is, we'll find him."

She nodded and prayed he was right. Eventually, somehow, they got on the subject of her decision to leave Kansas City.

"After I got sick, I didn't know what to do. Ricky was in school and didn't see what was happening. That meant I was able to keep it from him.

When I approached Rick about our son staying with him, he seemed great with it, and I thought Tiffany had matured enough to handle Ricky. He's really a great kid. It seemed the best option for him. I thought he'd be happy there. I thought after he didn't hear from me for a while, he'd be upset and maybe even hate me, but he'd transfer all his love and allegiance to his dad, and I was okay with that because Ricky would be happy. So I told Ricky I'd lost my job and had to find something else. I let the house go, paid off all the bills except the van, took what cash I had and tried to disappear."

"And landed in Buffalo Creek."

"You don't know how thankful I am for that," she exclaimed.

"Me, too," he said, and she knew he meant it—but maybe not for the same reasons she did.

They drove late into the night. Brooks urged her to rest, but she couldn't, really. He let her drive for a couple hours across Arkansas, where the highway stretched wide and long and dark. The hour had passed 2:00 a.m. when they reached the outskirts of Kansas City, Missouri. The temperature hovered just above twenty degrees, made colder by a stiff breeze blowing down from the north. By the time they crossed the river, traveled west and finally pulled up in front of Rick's Kansas home, the clock on the dashboard of the car read nine minutes until 3:00 o'clock in the morning.

Eva didn't waste a moment pounding on the door and getting Rick and Donita out of bed. Tiffany didn't bother to put in an appearance, but that didn't surprise Eva. The frown that her ex-husband gave Brooks did.

"Who's this?" he grumbled.

She hadn't realized how petulant and immature Rick could look compared to Brooks. They both had dark hair and light eyes, but one was definitely all man and the other was…of the same gender. Even wearing the dark shadow of a heavy beard with jeans and a simple pullover, Brooks looked polished and substantial, while Rick looked like a poser, a wannabe. Brooks stepped forward and held out his hand, introducing himself and, as always, taking the high road.

"Brooks Leland."

"*Doctor* Brooks Leland," Eva hastened to add.

"Eva's friend," Brooks added, hesitating just long enough between the two words to give weight to the word *friend*. She'd have loved him for that if she hadn't loved him already for everything he was and all he'd done. She wouldn't even lie to herself about it anymore. She loved him, plain and simple.

Rick frowned all the more, but Brooks just smiled pleasantly and shook hands.

Donita showed Eva and Brooks to Ricky's room, and they looked around until she found a notebook with Jared's name and an email address jotted down on the cover. Brooks used his smart phone to send an email right then, asking for information about Ricky and telling Jared that Ricky's mom was in town and where she could be found. Then nothing remained to be done except to throw herself on the uncertain mercy of her aunt. Even as tired and worried as she was, Eva couldn't help dreading that particular homecoming.

All her worst memories awaited her in that mean little house where she had grown up. This, she knew, would be the real test of her newfound faith, but she'd told Ricky's friends that was where she'd be. Besides, she didn't know where else to go. Most of her friends had drifted away after her divorce, and working from home made it difficult to make more, though it had undoubtedly been best for Ricky. She couldn't stay at Rick's, and she wouldn't ask Brooks to take her to a hotel, though he might well choose to find one for himself. In fact, she hoped he would. He needed to rest, and she didn't want to subject him to Aunt Donna's vitriol, but she didn't know how to tell him that without sounding ungrateful and critical. In the end, she was too tired to do more than trudge up the overgrown walk to knock on the cracked and faded paint of what had once been a Chinese red front door.

Donna did not disappoint. She answered, fully

dressed, with her usual sneering glance and a few clipped words but no greeting.

"Took you long enough."

Welcome home, Eva thought glumly. *How soon can I get out of here?*

"I expected you more than an hour ago," Eva's aunt grumbled.

A small, bony sixty-something woman with short white hair like densely packed boar bristles and Eva's green-hazel eyes, she turned abruptly from the door and paced into the small, dingy, cool living room. Eva sent Brooks an apologetic glance and followed. He went in behind her and pushed the door closed.

"Aunt Donna, this is Dr. Brooks Leland," Eva said.

Aunt Donna turned, her wrinkled lips fashioned in a seemingly permanent frown. She raked Brooks with a scathing gaze.

"Got you a doctor this time, did you? Well, don't think just because he's got a fancy title you can bring your fornication into this house."

Eva squeezed her eyes shut, sighing, "Aunt Donna."

Brooks laid a restraining hand on her shoulder, snapping, "I beg your pardon. You insult not just your niece with that remark but me."

"This is a Christian household," Donna began.

"I am a Christian," Brooks shot at her, "and

Eva's friend. Back home she has many Christian friends."

Donna seemed momentarily disarmed, but then she lifted her chin, looking down her slender nose at her niece. "Got them fooled, do you? Well, I know what sort you're drawn to. Look at that adulterer you married."

"That's on him!" Brooks erupted, instinctively parking his hands at his waist. It was an intimidation tactic, he knew, serving to make one look larger, and he already made two of the silly woman, but the stance kept him from reaching out to shake her. "Eva didn't cheat on him. It was the other way around. But you sound like you blame her."

"She chose him," Donna grumbled.

"And you have obviously chosen to punish her for his mistakes," Brooks shot back. He shook his head at Eva. "No wonder you didn't want to go to church when I first met you."

Eva flapped her arms. "What does that matter now with Ricky gone?"

"Ricky's gone?" Donna echoed.

"He ran away from his father's house," Eva revealed, sniffing.

Donna folded her hands. "Can't say I'm surprised. Rick Allenson is a disgrace to men everywhere, and you just blithely hand your son off to him."

"She did not," Brooks defended hotly. "She

tried to spare her son the same horror that she went through herself."

"Oh, please," Donna scoffed.

"She has her mother's disease," Brooks informed the old biddy. "She thought she was dying, and she didn't want her son to have to watch it."

For a long moment, Donna said nothing, but her clenched jaw gradually softened somewhat. "What do you mean?"

Eva crossed to the tweedy sofa, slipped off her coat and sank down, rubbing her temples. "Do we have to go into this now? I'm so tired."

"Yes, we do," Brooks said, glaring at Donna. "How old were you when your mother died, Eva?"

She shrugged. "Thirteen."

"So you weren't much older than Ricky when she became ill. Correct?"

"That's right."

"Meaning she was very near your age when she became ill, too." She blinked at him as if she'd just now considered that. "It is an inherited condition," he explained gently before asking, "Who took care of you then?"

"Aunt Donna. We always lived with Aunt Donna."

"So this was your only support system during your mother's illness and death," he said.

"Yes."

He went over and stood next to her, sliding his hand over her luxurious pale hair. "I'm sorry, sweetheart," he said gently. "I didn't really understand until now. You were very much alone, weren't you?"

"I had Ava," she said in a quivering voice.

"Your twin."

"Yes."

"How old were you when she died?"

"Twenty-two."

"Just twenty-two. And when you married?"

"Twenty-four."

"And you had Ricky at twenty-five," he said, amazed that she'd waited even those two years to marry, as alone as she must have been.

"Ask her how old she was when she and her sister left home," Donna insisted self-righteously. "Just ask her."

"Eighteen," Eva said firmly. "We left the very day we graduated from high school."

"Ungrateful, wild, willful," Donna pronounced. "Couldn't wait to meet boys and wear their short skirts and—"

"Escape your hatred," Brooks interrupted smoothly. Donna looked stunned.

"I treated them like my own!" Donna insisted.

"Perhaps you did," Brooks said. "That doesn't mean you loved them."

"Love us?" Eva whispered. "She hated us. Ava wouldn't even see her when she was dying."

"I didn't hate you!" Donna cried. "I wanted

to…make amends, but she wouldn't let me. She shut me out."

"You shut us out," Eva accused tiredly. "You always shut us out."

"I don't understand," Brooks said. "Most women love their sister's children."

Her face suddenly contorted. "How could I love them? My sister and my husband's children but not mine!"

"What?" Eva looked at her as if she'd lost her mind.

"She really never told you?" Donna demanded. "Not even on her deathbed she didn't have the nerve to confess what she'd done? Seducing my husband away from me!"

A heavy silence filled the room, the kind that follows an explosion.

Chapter Thirteen

"Mama was *sixteen* when we were born," Eva exclaimed.

"Old enough to know better," Donna insisted. "I took her in when our mother died, and how did she repay me? My husband and I were grieving that we couldn't have children when she crawled into his bed, then the two of you were born!"

"What you really mean," Brooks stated flatly, "is that while *you* were grieving because *you* couldn't have children, your husband crawled into your little sister's bed."

"And then ran off as soon as her condition became obvious," Donna wailed, "leaving me to raise his mistakes!"

Eva fell back on the sofa, her hands slapped to her head. Brooks sat down, sad and weary to his bones, and gathered her into his arms. "And you've punished Eva, her sister and their mother for his sins ever since."

"Visiting the iniquity of the fathers upon the children, and upon the children's children," Donna began quoting.

"Oh, stop it," Brooks scolded. "You can misapply Exodus all you want, but it doesn't justify your attitude and behavior. What about Mark? 'And when you stand praying, if you hold anything against anyone, forgive them, so that your Father in Heaven may forgive you your sins.' Or would you rather be angry than forgiven?"

"Mama *died*," Eva wept, "and what life did she ever really have? She worked and she stayed home with us. That's all she ever did until she got sick, and then she s-suffered. You made sure of that! You made sure she knew she was a burden and a bother the whole time she was sick. I used to hear her praying to have it over with! And I didn't want Ricky to see me like that."

"Ricky will never see you like that," Brooks promised, holding her tight. "Even if the surgery doesn't work—and I have every confidence that it will—your son will never go through what you have. He'll never be alone or unloved or friendless. I promise you."

"Blzzllgull," Eva said, suddenly looking panicked. "Awlzekhub!"

"No!" Brooks exclaimed. "Oh, sweetheart, I'm sorry. I was afraid of this."

"Shuntlefewk!" she cried, shaking her head as he eased away and rose.

"It's all right," he told her, moving toward the door. "I came prepared. Wait here, and try to stay calm." He ran out to the car, glad he hadn't removed his overcoat, and grabbed the blue travel bag, sprinting back to the house with it.

Donna sat on the edge of the sofa, awkwardly patting Eva's hand. She slumped in the corner, her eyes half-closed, her breathing shallow. Brooks had tried to see to it that she stayed hydrated during the trip, but her obvious exhaustion tore at him. He fell to his knees next to her and quickly assembled the IV pole, then tied a tourniquet around her biceps and plumped up a vein before pulling on gloves and opening up the IV kit. Only after he had the medication flowing and the bag hanging on the pole did he take her blood pressure, perform a cursory examination and then inject a second medication into the IV line.

"You just need to rest, sweetheart," he told her, smoothing her glorious hair away from her beautiful face. "You're exhausted. The medication will take the pressure off, and sleep will renew your strength. When you wake, everything will be better. Then we'll go bring your son home. Until then, I'll be here praying."

"I will, too," Donna said quietly, and Brooks saw Eva's hand squeeze hers. He had no idea what had passed between them in the few moments he had been gone, but they seemed to have reached an uneasy peace for the moment.

Eva lifted a weary gaze to meet his and mumbled, "Zzllttll."

Somehow, he knew exactly what she meant, and he chuckled to show her that her worries were for naught. "I'll rest, too. Promise."

She closed her eyes, but then her aunt burbled, "Oh, Eva, I'm so sorry!"

Eva sighed. "Koogilltay."

"She knows," Brooks said, smiling as her eyes at last drifted closed. He'd never before realized how blond her lashes were and how very thick, like tiny curved brushes.

Dear God, he thought, *how I love this woman! Thank You. No matter what happens, thank You for bringing her to me.*

Injecting the IV line with a mild sedative was a dirty trick, and he might well pay for it later, but Brooks would not risk Eva's health further. She needed sleep, and she was going to get it. After the small med bag emptied, he had Donna turn down a bed for Eva and carried her to it. Then he stretched out on another bed, fully clothed, in another cold, dingy room in the small house and prayed himself to sleep.

He woke a few hours later to the smell of coffee and padded into the kitchen, the only truly warm room in the place. Donna actually made him breakfast and let him use the shower. Clean, shaved and freshly dressed, he returned phone calls and sat alone on the sofa in the living room answering emails via his smart phone until Eva finally wandered in, looking rumpled and sad, about one o'clock in the afternoon.

She came straight to the sofa, crawled up onto it, looped her arms about his neck and laid her head on his shoulder, whispering, "He hasn't called. I checked my phone, and I called Chatam House just to be sure he didn't try to reach me there. The police haven't come up with anything, either."

"We'll find him," Brooks said, kissing the top of her head. "How do you feel?"

"Okay. Better. Miserable. What did you give me?"

"A sedative. I won't do it again without your permission. Let's get some coffee in you, then you can shower while I find you something to eat."

She sighed. "Might as well."

"Then we'll go pack Ricky's things," Brooks said. She lifted her head, a slight crease between her brows. "He's going home with us," Brooks pointed out. "Might as well be ready. Right?"

She smiled wanly. "Right."

"Then we'll talk to Ricky's friends, actually go see them. They ought to be home from school by the time we've finished the packing."

"You've thought about this, planned it all out."

He nodded. "I emailed Jared, asked for an address. Haven't heard back yet, but the kid's got to check his email sometime."

She wrapped her arms around his neck again nd kissed him right behind his ear, giving him big grin and lovely shivers all the way down to is toes. "Thank you. For everything."

He patted her knee as nonchalantly as he could nanage. "Come on. Aunt Donna is not Hilda, but he coffee is good."

Eva didn't hurry, and Brooks saw no reason o rush her. When she was ready, they stopped ff to pick up some boxes and drove over to the Allenson house. Dorinda let them in, confirmed hat they had heard nothing from Ricky and disppeared without a word when Eva stated their ntention to pack up Ricky's things. To Brooks's urprise, however, Rick Sr. showed up about half n hour later. He stopped in the doorway and eaned a shoulder against the jamb, glowering at hem. Eva gave him no more than a cursory glance s she folded Ricky's clothes.

"You're obviously not here to stop us," she bserved.

"No."

"Just making sure we don't take anything of alue to you, then."

"Look, Eva," Rick snapped, "he's done nothing ut complain since you left him here."

"Really? Well, I suppose he was used to having a parent around."

"That's not fair," Rick insisted. "You didn't ave anyone to concentrate on but him."

Brooks felt his jaw drop, but he managed t keep his tongue still as Eva slowly turned to fac her ex.

"So you're saying that you can't manage hav ing two people in your life at one time."

Allenson pinched his nose. "It's not that. Th thing is, my wife is simply too young to raise ten-year-old."

Brooks could not resist. "Well, then she's to young to be married to you, isn't she, seeing a how you *have* a ten-year-old. I mean, he was o the scene before she was. Right?"

Rick glared at him, but then he turned and le them, snarling, "Take anything you want. Tak the furniture!"

Eva sent Brooks a taut smile. He shook hi head. "Sorry. None of my business."

"You didn't say anything that wasn't perfectl true."

They finished packing and closing up the boxe Finally, Eva slung on her coat.

"Let's go find my boy."

Nightfall brought the very lowest ebb in Eva spirits thus far. She'd felt sure that visiting Ricky friends in person would yield positive results. did not. They had even gone to Ricky's new scho in hopes of learning who Jared might be, as he ha not answered either of their emails, but the scho ould only promise to speak to Ricky's teachers, one of whom had seen him in two full days now.

Eva had never felt like such a failure. How ould she have been so stupid as to leave her precious son with her idiot ex? What if something ad happened to Ricky? He could be dead in an lley somewhere. Even smart boys did stupid nings, made bad choices. If that were not so, he'd ave waited until she came for him. Of course, if he were not stupid, she'd have told him why she ouldn't come, which led her right back to her ailures as a mother.

Then again, how could she have been so stupid as to accept at face value a decades-old prognosis and simply give up on her life and, in the rocess, her son, on that basis? It had all been so eartbreakingly pointless. And yet she had met Brooks and the Chatams because of it. In a very eal way, she had met Jesus Christ because of it. o why was she so scared?

"It's going to be all right," Brooks said for peraps the hundredth time.

"Is it?" she asked wearily. "Where could he e? And even if we find him, what happens to im if I die?"

"Hush," Brooks told her. "Don't talk like that. Don't even think it."

"How can I help it? I've been such an abysmal ailure as a mother."

"Stop it."

"Why else did he run away?"

"He was unhappy, and he wanted to punish yo
and his father for making him unhappy. That
why he ran away."

"What if something's happened to him?"

"Then, we'll cross that bridge when we com
to it," Brooks said, "but I refuse to believe it unt
it's proved to me."

"What if we never know?"

"We'll know. Sooner or later, one day we'
know."

"I can't bear it, Brooks."

"No one could, but God can, and He will bea
it for you. I've had experience at this, Eva, and s
have you. We survive the unsurvivable becaus
God comes alongside us and helps us bear the bur
den. He has experience at this, too, you know, los
ing those He loves. It happens to Him every day

"I never thought of that before."

"Every time a person rejects God, every time
person dies with that rejection on his or her sou
God grieves, just as He rejoices every time on
of us chooses Him."

"I wish that made me feel better," she said, "bu
it just makes me feel sad for Him."

"I understand, but God wants us to focus o
the joy, Eva, and when you're well, we'll be abl
to do that. In the meantime, the thing that alway
makes me feel better is prayer. Come here, an
let us pray together."

"I'd like that."

They settled into the corner of the sofa. Where Aunt Donna had gotten off to Eva neither knew nor cared. With Brooks's arm around her, she settled against his shoulder and closed her eyes as he began to softly speak.

"Father God, thank You for bringing Eva and her son into my life. Wherever Ricky is, please keep him safe and bring him back to his mom well and whole soon…"

"Yes, Lord," she whispered.

Brooks went on speaking, and she did find comfort in sharing that prayer with him, so much so that when the amens were said she did not move. Neither did Brooks. In fact, he snuggled down and put his feet up on the rickety old coffee table that Donna kept sitting to one side. Eva sighed and closed her eyes, and the next thing she knew it was morning. Somehow, she'd gotten stretched out on the sofa and covered by a blanket, and someone was knocking on the door.

She heard Donna flipping the locks and rubbed her eyes, looking up to find Brooks standing in the doorway to the tiny hall in his stocking feet. He needed a shave and a comb and wore the same clothes as the day before. She pushed up onto her elbow, loving him with an empty, aching, bottomless need that told her she had never truly loved any man before him. Suddenly, she could forgive Rick his infidelity, for if Tiffany was able to love

him with one-tenth of what she felt for Brooks
then she could give Rick more than Eva had been
able to give him. She heard Donna speaking bu
had no idea what she'd said, then suddenly Brook
stood very straight, grinning, and she realized
someone else had come into the room.

"Ricky?" Brooks asked, as Eva jackknifed into
a sitting position, and there he was, her beautiful
stupid, wonderful, exasperating son, accompanied
by an adult couple she'd never before seen.

She opened her arms and started to cry. He
dropped his backpack and practically fell onto
her, crying, "Mom!"

"I'm so sorry, Mrs. Allenson," said the man, a
tall pudgy fellow with features too small for his
big square head.

Eva cleared her throat and tried not to bawl
"It's Russell. Eva Russell. And I don't know wha
you're apologizing for. You've brought my son to
me. Thank you."

They were Jared's parents, of course, Darrer
and Lois Hollis. Mr. Hollis explained that he had
been out of town on business, returning only the
evening before, Saturday, and Jared was not al
lowed to use the computer when his father wa
not at home, so he hadn't seen the emails unti
that morning. Mrs. Hollis told the real tale, how
ever. Ricky and Jared had convinced her that his
parents had been called out of town unexpectedly
so he needed to stay at Jared's house.

"I tried to call the number that he gave me," Lois Hollis, a little wren of a woman, said, "but had been disconnected. Ricky claimed they'd een having trouble paying the bill."

Eva looked at Ricky, who had bowed his head. You gave them our old number, didn't you?" Ie nodded, and Eva sighed. "Mrs. Hollis, I'm so orry. Ricky didn't want to live with his father and tepmother any longer and was impatient for me come and get him. That's all this was. I can't ll you how frantic we've been or how grateful I m to you for looking out for him."

"Well, he did seem to be unsupervised a great eal."

"So I've been told." She looked at Ricky and aid, "But that has come to an end."

"I was especially worried because he was too ick to attend school," the woman said.

Eva lifted her eyebrows and looked to Brooks, vho was still grinning. "I'll get my bag."

"Dr. Leland will take care of him," she said, as Brooks disappeared into the hallway, "if there's nything wrong with him, that is."

Ricky turned red all the way to his shaggy dark airline.

"We need to go if we're not going to be late for hurch," Mr. Hollis said.

"I cannot thank you enough," Eva told him, etting to her feet and walking them to the door.

Impulsively, she hugged Mrs. Hollis. "God bles
you both."

The woman smiled and nodded as they left.

Eva turned to her son, giddy with relief. "You,'
she said, shaking her finger at him, "should than
God that I'm so happy to see you I'm not hangin
you by your toes."

"Mom," he began defensively, "you have n
idea how bad it was at Dad's."

"Yes, I do, and that's no excuse. You shoul
have waited until I could come."

"If you couldn't come, then how come you'r
here?" he argued.

"You've no idea what you're saying," Brook
said, carrying his physician's bag to the coffe
table.

Ricky rounded on him. "What business is i
of yours?"

"I'm her doctor," Brooks answered, reachin
into his bag. "It's every bit my business when yo
put her *very fragile health* in *further jeopardy*
Open your mouth."

"Wha—" Ricky began, at which point Brook
shoved a tongue depressor into his mouth an
looked down his throat. "...are you talkin
about?" Ricky gasped when the little wood pad
dle was removed.

"Your mother," Brooks said, turning Ricky'
head to peer into his ear with a lighted scope, "ha
a cyst in her brain."

"Huh?"

He turned Ricky's head and checked his other ear. "She was misdiagnosed by a doctor here who thought she had a brain tumor." He stowed the scope and brought out a digital fever thermometer, which he raked across Ricky's forehead and down his cheek. "She thought she was dying when she left you with your father, and she wasn't wrong. He might be dead now if we hadn't figured out the real issue."

Ricky gasped. "Mom!" He threw his arms round Eva.

"He's fine," Brooks told her. Then he dropped hand onto Ricky's shoulder. "She's going to be ne, too. We're going to take her home to Texas nd give her an operation, and she's going to get well. Okay?"

Ricky shuddered and looked up at him. "Are you sure?"

"As sure as I can be."

"But what if she's not?" he wailed.

Brooks squeezed his shoulder. "You'll still be kay." He smiled. "I like ten-year-old boys, and have these cool friends. Some of them are old, ut they're cool. You'll like them." And Eva fell n love with him all over again. He had as much s offered to adopt her son just then, and she had very intention of letting him do so, should any-hing happen to her. Maybe this was what the

whole thing had been about. Maybe this was th
point of it all.

"I guess we should get on the road," she sai
stroking Ricky's dark hair. She realized that h
could pass for her and Brooks's son in a heartbea

"What about my stuff?" Ricky asked.

"It's in the trunk of my car," Brooks told hin

"We packed it up yesterday," Eva said.

"Think you could delay long enough to atten
early service with me?" Donna asked uncertainl

Eva glanced at her aunt in surprise, then looke
to Brooks. He shrugged.

"I like church."

"I don't have many clothes with me," Ev
warned.

"It's casual," Donna said, "but we'd have to g
a move on."

Eva smiled. "What are we waiting for?"

She had more than enough time to worship
God so loving that He would provide such a ma
for her son.

They took their time on the trip back to Texa
Ricky talked a mile a minute for the first sever:
hours. Eva let him gab, basking in the sound of h
voice. The two of them had always spent a lot c
time talking, and she had missed that like craz:
She hadn't realized that he didn't have that sam
kind of communication with his dad. Apparentl
Rick remained a workaholic and thought their so

ught to be happy with a shared video game now
nd again. With Ricky living in the house, his dad
ad felt free to take his twice monthly weekends
way with adult friends, so instead of having more
f his dad, by moving in with him, Ricky had ac-
ually had less. It seemed not to have occurred to
'iffany that if she kept to her own schedule, Ricky
vould be home alone. If not for Donita, he'd have
een completely without adult supervision most
f the time.

Ricky hadn't minded his new school, and his
grades hadn't suffered significantly because he
vas one of those kids who liked school, not that
is dad had noticed, apparently. During her visit
here, Eva had let the school know that she in-
ended to enroll him in an out-of-state system
oon, and the administration had promised to
ave his records ready for electronic transfer.
Ricky seemed a little nervous about the com-
ng change—another school in a short period of
ime—but Brooks assured him that Buffalo Creek
oasted a number of good schools, both public and
rivate, all the way through college.

"We'll find a good fit for you," Brooks prom-
sed. "I know a lot of the administrators and teach-
rs."

Surprisingly, Ricky had a good many questions
or Brooks. Many of them had to do with Eva's
ondition and upcoming surgery, but he asked

even more about the practice of medicine and the some embarrassingly personal ones.

"You got any kids?"

"Nope."

"How come?"

"My wife died before we could have any."

"Then, how do you know you like 'em?"

"I've met a lot of kids over the years. Can't remember any I didn't like."

"But you haven't lived with any, have you? Ricky pressed.

"No, I haven't."

"So how do you know you'd like living with a kid?"

"I never lived with a woman before I got married—other than my mother, that is—but I knew I'd like living with my wife, and I did."

Ricky screwed up his face. "I'm confused. Does that mean you like living with my mom?"

Brooks shot a glance across the front seat to Eva, who snapped, "Ricky! We're not living together."

"But Dad said you were most likely shacked up with some guy and—"

Eva gasped and twisted in her seat to look at him over her shoulder. "Have you ever known me to 'shack up' with anyone?"

"N-no, but—"

"I've barely dated since the divorce, Ricky."

"That's 'cause I was around," he said softly.

"You thought you were in my way?" she asked, horrified. "No! That's not why I left."

"Ricky, your mother is not sleeping with me," Brooks stated bluntly. "You insult us both by assuming she is. That's not behavior in which moral, Christian people engage outside of marriage. She tried to do a very selfless thing. Her leaving hurt you, but she was trying to spare you a greater pain. She didn't want you to watch her die. She thought you enjoyed being with your father and that you'd be happy with him. Thankfully, her prognosis was wrong, and she has a very good chance of beating this so the two of you can be together."

"Then, you're, like, just her doctor?" Ricky asked, sounding disappointed.

Brooks shifted in his seat. "Not exactly."

"I work for Dr. Leland," Eva put in quickly. "We're friends. Good friends."

Brooks sent her an unreadable look. Finally he said, "Your mother is very dear to me, for several reasons, so by extension, you're dear to me, too."

"What's that mean?" Ricky asked suspiciously.

"It means that I'm ready to like you just because you're her son, but I hope you and I will like each other apart from her, that we'll have our own friendship."

"Oh."

The boy fell quiet after that, until he got hungry, and they stopped for dinner. He seemed uncertain how to behave around Brooks still, and Eva told herself that it would take time for him to get to know the good doctor the way she did. She prayed that when that day came, she would be there to see it.

Chapter Fourteen

Eva spent the remainder of the trip trying to prepare Ricky for Chatam House. The idea of elderly
triplets tickled him, but he couldn't wrap his mind
around living anywhere with a cook, a maid and
a houseman.

"They are *not* servants," Eva instructed him.
"They are staff, and if you don't treat them with
the utmost respect, I will confine you to our room
until I can find us someplace else to go. Got it?"

"Got it."

"A word of advice," Brooks said. "The Chatams
are old-fashioned dears. You'd do well to address
everyone in that house as sir and ma'am. Think
you can remember that?"

"Yes…sir."

Brooks grinned into the rearview mirror. "I
knew you were a smart boy. One more thing.
Miss Hypatia has been very ill and is recovering
from major surgery. Chatam House is big, but

you'll need to keep the noise down, especially
when you're on the stairs or in the dining room."

Ricky nodded soberly, as if committing this
all to memory.

"Oh, say," Brooks went on, "you don't like
hockey by any chance, do you?"

"Sure!" He launched into a recitation of his favorite team's players and their stats.

"What do you think of Stephen Gallow?"
Brooks asked.

Ricky frowned. "Man, that dude is bad news.
He completely ruined our chances in the play-offs
last year. I hate that guy!"

"You don't want to meet him then?"

Ricky's eyes got huge. "You *know* him?"

"He's married to a Chatam niece and lives
in Buffalo Creek, but if you don't want to meet
him…"

"No! I—I mean, yes! Steve Gallow? He's one
of the best goalies in the league!"

"Okay," Brooks said nonchalantly, winking
at Eva, who bit her lips to keep from laughing.
"We'll set up something."

"Steve Gallow," Ricky exclaimed, clapping his
hands to his head in amazement.

"Score one for the doctor," Eva whispered, and
Brooks chuckled.

Thanks to the hockey star reference, Ricky
seemed appropriately awed by the time they
reached Chatam House. Eva gave her whole-

hearted permission for Carol and Chester to move her things into the East Suite, so she and Ricky could have separate bedrooms. Chester met them in the foyer, and everyone else but Hypatia, Carol and Hilda awaited them in the front parlor.

Eva ushered her son into the large fussy room, Brooks at their heels. Ricky goggled at Odelia's purple-and-yellow striped jumper, matching turban and fist-sized sun disc earrings, but it was Kent's hot pink vest and red bow tie that made his eyebrows leap. He got through the introductions without embarrassing her, however. Then Magnolia asked if he would like a cup of tea.

He wrinkled his nose but politely said, "No, thank you. Ma'am."

"Some cookies and cakes, then?"

"Yeah, sure."

"Why don't you sit on the floor?" Eva suggested, and he went to his knees right there next to the table. Magnolia passed him a linen napkin, and after a slightly puzzled pause he spread it across his lap as he began downing cookies.

Eva sat beside Brooks on an armless chair in front of the fireplace and accepted a cup of tea and a plate of tiny cakes, listening while Brooks caught up on Hypatia's condition. After emptying his own cup, he set aside his plate and rose, saying, "I'll just go up and check in on her before I leave."

"The nurse is with her," Magnolia informed him with a nod.

Eva decided that she and Ricky would go with him. "I don't want to interrupt her evening more than once. Besides, we're ready to turn in."

Kent volunteered to help Chester with the remaining boxes, so Eva and Ricky climbed the stairs with Brooks. Ricky stared, openmouthed at the marble staircase, ceiling and woodwork. When they reached the landing, Brooks led them to the suite belonging to Hypatia and Magnolia. He knocked and waited until a smiling, middle-aged female nurse with short fading red hair came to let them in and led them across the sitting room to Hypatia's bedroom. The antique bed had been replaced with a modern hospital one.

Hypatia looked much better. Brooks smiled at her. She held out both hands. He clasped them and sat down on the edge of her bed to kiss her cheek.

"I'm glad to see you so improved."

"Off to play knight errant, were you?"

"What's night errand?" Ricky asked, prompting Hypatia to look around Brooks.

"Eva, dear." She nodded at Ricky. "This, I take it, is your son."

Eva smiled proudly. "Richard Russell Allenson. We call him Ricky."

"How do you do, young man? Richard is a more stately name and will serve you better in a few years, I have no doubt. You're a handsome rascal."

"Thank you, ma'am," Ricky rasped, not stumbling at all over the honorific this time. "I won't run on the stairs, I promise," he added.

She smiled. "I appreciate that. Thank you."

"We'll let you rest now," Brooks told her. "We just wanted to say hello."

"Pish posh," she retorted. "I've done little but rest since I got home."

He chuckled. "Then, let *us* rest. It's been quite a weekend, and we have to enroll this boy in school tomorrow."

Hypatia reached out her hands and cupped Brooks's cheeks, staring into his eyes. Whatever she saw there made them both smile. After a moment, he leaned forward and kissed her forehead. Then he got to his feet. Hypatia looked to Ricky.

"I trust you'll come and tell me all about your first day of school tomorrow."

Ricky glanced at his mom in surprise before answering. "Yes, ma'am."

"And no more of this running away and scaring everyone half to death. A man stands his ground, Richard. Remember that."

"Yes, ma'am."

"I'll see you tomorrow afternoon."

"Yes, ma'am."

"I look forward to it."

Brooks smiled at Eva, sliding his arm across her shoulders and turning her back into the sitting room. "That's just how she got to me," he whispered. "Soon he'll put out his eyes before disappointing her."

Sure he was right, Eva thought, *Finally, I've done the right thing for my son.*

Correction: *God* had brought her to the right place and showed her the right things to do. Beyond grateful, she would not ask for more.

Brooks advised enrolling Ricky in the Parkhurst School. The Parkhurst school had a slight edge over the other options because the class sizes in Ricky's grade were slightly smaller. Brooks had occasion to know this, he said, because he happened to live in the Parkhurst neighborhood. That settled the issue for Eva.

They had Ricky enrolled by 10:00 a.m., with Brooks as the secondary contact after Eva herself. Then, thanks to Magnolia, they met Asher Chatam, the attorney, for lunch at Chatam House. He agreed to draw up papers allowing Brooks to take formal custody of Ricky in the event of Eva's death or mental incapacity. They anticipated no argument from Rick on the matter.

"But it won't come to that," Brooks insisted.

"You know the risks," Eva said, "and they are significant."

"We have one of the best surgeons in the country," he pointed out, "and lots of prayer."

She nodded and let it go at that. "What we need now is a barber."

"How so?" Asher asked, obviously puzzled.

Eva flipped a hank of her long hair at him. "Have to whack this off." She tried not to sound sick about it. "In case they have to shave my head."

"She just has too much hair," Brooks added regretfully, sliding his hand over her head, "but it'll grow back."

"I'll have Ellie call you," Asher said. "My wife has a head full of crazy curls. She'll know the best place to go."

"I'd appreciate that very much," Eva told him. "In fact, I appreciate everything the Chatams have done for me and my son more than I can ever say. Dying in Buffalo Creek is like finding a bonanza."

Instead of laughing, Asher looked startled, but Brooks chuckled.

"Ignore her," he advised, sliding an arm across the top of her dining chair. "She jokes when she's scared spitless."

"Beats bawling," Eva groused.

"She does *that* when she's happy, angry or embarrassed," Brooks said to Asher, "and when she's tired she speaks gibberish, but we're going to fix that on Wednesday."

She punched him in the ribs, a short, neat jab that surprised an "oof" out of him, which finally made Asher laugh.

"Remind me to keep her away from Ellie," he teased.

"Oh, right," Brooks groaned, rubbing his side,

"so says the man married to the soccer coach who wears tutus and floppy ears."

Asher grinned as he slid back his chair. "Welcome to my world, Doctor. Glorious, isn't it?"

"I'll let you know," Brooks muttered.

"Papers will be ready tomorrow afternoon," Asher promised, checking his wristwatch.

Eva spent the next few hours answering and making phone calls while unpacking Ricky's things so he'd feel comfortable in the room he'd chosen as his own. By the time Brooks picked him up from school and returned to Chatam House with him, she had everything shipshape, and appointments with a beautician and a wig maker for the next morning.

Ricky was full of stories about his day. The kids were mostly nice, especially when they found out he was staying at Chatam House. He liked his teacher, and could he play soccer in the spring? He had to study *Texas* history at some point. And he had a different teacher for math. Ricky liked math. Eva and Brooks took him in to visit with Hypatia and found themselves summarily dismissed.

"It's all right," Brooks assured her, escorting her out of the sisters' suite. "Hypatia has much experience dealing with boys."

"But he doesn't have much experience dealing with Hypatia," Eva muttered.

Brooks chuckled. "It'll be fine."

"That's become your favorite refrain. It'll be

fine. It'll be okay. It'll be all right. I'm going to set it to music and teach you to tap dance."

"How do you know I don't tap dance already?"

"Do you?"

He smiled. "Of course not. Do you write music?"

"As well as you tap dance."

"Sounds like a perfect pairing."

"Now who's the jokester," she grumbled, but he just laughed.

"Time for your meds."

"And a nag, too," she muttered, but she couldn't talk herself out of loving the man no matter how hopeless it was.

Tomorrow she was going to have her hair cut off so the next day she could have her head shaved and her skull cracked open, and then who knew what would happen? She could be completely well in a matter of days, or permanently impaired. Or dead. Or dying, just as she was now. But at least her son's future was secured, and she had a fighting chance for more.

Not by sound or sign would Brooks show the depth of regret he felt when the stylist began to cut Eva's beautiful hair. He could have kissed the woman, however, when she insisted on ignoring Eva's goofy instruction not to bother styling her "massive mop" as it would likely be shaved anyway. Instead, she sculpted Eva's pale blond locks into a chic chin-length bob that showed off the elegant length of Eva's neck and framed her lovely face. She suggested that they keep the foot-long locks of Eva's hair to have a wig made for her in case the surgeon did have to shave Eva's head. Brooks found that suggestion imminently logical and came away from the appointment with Eva's shorn hair in a plastic bag, which he carried with them to the wig maker's. There, all the while joking, Eva purchased a wig very like her own hair in its current style and color, though anyone who knew her would see the difference. She also chose a pageboy style to be made of her own hair, should that prove necessary, and then she and Brooks went to Asher's office to sign the papers he'd drawn up for her—living will, custody papers and power of attorney—so he could take care of Ricky and her if she couldn't. After that, she let Brooks drive her into Dallas to the hospital.

They had arranged for Chester to pick up Ricky after school. Since it came with a driver, to Ricky the town car was a limo. He was thrilled, and if the affectation helped subdue his anxiety over his mother's hospital stay and surgery, the adults were all of a mind to indulge the fantasy. The aunties would oversee his homework, dinner and bedtime, and between those events they had arranged some company about his own age.

A battery of tests had been ordered for Eva, and Brooks accompanied her to them all, charming or barging his way in to get a look at the results as they came in, though he was no neurosurgeon. He didn't know what to look for beyond a certain point, and he didn't question the surgeon's purpose or ability. So he kept his opinions to himself and concentrated on Eva. He'd become quite adept at playing straight man to her comic, interpreting her zingers for the medical staff and laughing with just the right mixture of lightheartedness and concern to let them know that her fear of dying or impairment was real and could still be taken with the proverbial grain of salt.

When she finally fell into a sound sleep, he felt utterly exhausted himself, but leaving her there alone the night before the surgery and going home was something he simply could not do. For the first time he truly understood what it was like to be on the other side of the white coat. He hadn't left Brigitte's side in the hospital because he'd known it was the end, but no treatment had been involved other than the palliative. This was entirely different. This hope felt as painful in its own way as had the certainty of Brigitte's death, and no way could he leave Eva alone with it. He asked for a toothbrush and blanket and sacked out in the recliner in her room, deciding within the hour that whoever thought those things were a fitting option for patients' rooms had a malevolent streak.

He woke well before she did, if he ever really slept, and was able to call Morgan to ask for a change of clothes and his electric razor. The surgeon came by, and they had a nice, long chat, which pleased Brooks immensely, and then the anesthesiologist came in, and Brooks had to wake her. She stretched lazily beneath his hand on her shoulder and smiled up at him.

"Hello, you."

He realized suddenly that he longed to wake up to that greeting every morning and knew that once this was over, he would ask her to marry him. But once this was over, she would have every option open to her, and perhaps the gratitude she was feeling now wouldn't become the love for which he hoped and prayed. He had told himself that if she lived and was whole, that would be enough, but he'd lied to himself once before when Brigitte and Morgan had announced their engagement. He'd told himself then that if the two people he loved most in the world were happy, he would be happy, but his heart had broken, and he'd feared that what they'd all had would forever be ruined because he would forever love his best friend's wife. He would try to be happy without her, just as he would have tried to be happy for Brigitte and Morgan, but God would have to find a way to work this out because, as before, Brooks did not have this in him.

Suddenly he feared what that plan might entail. For her.

I will gladly accept any suffering and disap-

pointment for myself, Lord, he silently prayed, *but please, please, spare her.*

That smile was something a woman could wake up to every morning of her life, Eva thought, if she had a life.

Lord, I said I wouldn't ask for anything more, Eva prayed. *I lied. I want this man for myself as well as my son, and I don't just want him, I want You to make me the very best thing that ever happened to him, everything he could ever have wished for and more, everything You could want for him.*

"Eva," Brooks said, "the anesthesiologist is here to speak to you. He has some important information for you."

Eva realized Brooks had spent the night at the hospital, and she wanted both to scold him and to hug him for that. Instead, she sat up in bed and tried to listen as the anesthesiologist terrified her with warnings about nerve blocks and spinal blocks, wire cages for her head, mechanical chairs and positions.

"I'll be *awake*," Eva screeched, "but immobilized? Talk about your nightmare scenarios!"

"I'll be right there with you," Brooks promised. "I'm scrubbing up and sitting in. I'll be holding your hand throughout."

"Bring a mallet," she suggested dryly. "I have a

feeling I'm going to want to give someone a drubbing before we're done."

He chuckled. The other doctor droned on about why this was all necessary, about the delicacy of the surgery and everything that could go haywire until she covered her ears and demanded, "Is he trying to make me back out of this?"

Brooks gently pulled her hands away, saying, "No, sweetheart, he has to say these things. Listen now while I tell you the good news. The cyst doesn't appear to be solid. It appears to be filled with fluid."

"That's good news?"

"It is. It means the cyst itself is less serious than we feared. Also, if they can get to it in the way they hope, they won't have to shave your head, just a space about the size of a half dollar. They may have to put a little shunt in to keep it from forming again, but that's done all the time. It's a little trickier to do it this way, but the surgeon's confident. It's up to you, though. They can shave your head and actually crack your skull instead of cutting a hole in it."

"Hey, what's another hole more or less?" she joked. Then she formed a megaphone with her hands and bleated, "Save the hair!" Grinning, Brooks shook his head, so she kept it up. "Isn't there a female rights group we can contact? Women Thou Art Vanity, or something like that?"

"Stop it," he told her. "We're talking about recovery times versus risk ratios here."

"So, more hair and less recovery time versus slightly higher risk, right?"

"That's it exactly."

She held up her hand. "I vote for more hair and less recovery time."

"Your vote is the only one that counts," Brooks told her, nodding at the anesthesiologist, who nodded at Eva and tapped notes in his tablet.

The next few hours both flew and dragged. Techs showed up to set up IVs in both her arms. Morgan and Lyla came with a razor and clothing for Brooks. He shaved but then took the fresh clothing with him for later use. Morgan and Lyla did their best to entertain her until he returned in the ubiquitous green pajama-like uniform that all surgery personnel seemed to wear. Unfortunately, the surgeon was running "slightly behind."

Eva wanted to scream. Instead, she joked. She joked about her hair. She joked about her ex. She joked about being hungry because she was. She joked about Ricky and his "limo ride" from school. When she got to the point of joking about Lyla's ex and her bout with cancer, she succumbed to tears, and it was then a nurse with a wheelchair finally entered the room.

They wheeled her off through hallways and elevators to pre-op. Just outside of double metal doors, Morgan and Lyla left them to gesture through a glass wall to the waiting room beyond. Shocked to see the crowd spilling out into the hallway, Eva felt her tears start again. Odelia and Kent were there, along with Magnolia and Pastor Hub, Carissa and Phillip Chatam, Reeves and Anna Leland in all her glorious pregnancy, Kaylie and Stephen Gallow, Petra and Dale Bowen, Asher and Ellie Chatam, even Garrett and Bethany Willows.

Eva wanted to say something clever but she couldn't speak, so she just wiped away her tears and nodded, smiling.

"Let us have a moment," Brooks said to the nurse, while everyone gathered around. "Hub, would you?"

"Of course." The elderly pastor cleared his throat and began to pray.

A few moments later, Brooks crouched before her, threaded his big capable hands through her hair and said, "Remember that tap dance, sweetheart. It will be okay. One way or another, it will be just fine, and I'll be with you, all the way. This is just for courage." And he kissed her, right there in front of all his friends. Quite a thorough job he did of it, too. No quick smack of the lips or gentle bussing, this was a blatant statement, a deep, ardent claiming, a solemn promise and as mind-boggling as any drug. Her eyes hadn't uncrossed before the nurse pushed her through those metal doors, Brooks calling out behind her, "I'll be along soon."

She didn't see him again until they wheeled her into the surgery theater sometime later. He met her at the door, smiling behind his mask. They were both outfitted as if they were going to perform the surgery themselves. She had been scrubbed and medicated from head to toe, but the hair shaving didn't take place until she was strapped into the chair, tilted at an awkward but surprisingly comfortable angle and clasped, latex glove to latex glove, by Brooks. The shaving felt more like suctioning, which was interesting, and she felt nothing when they cut the flap in her scalp, but no one prepared her for the excruciating sound of the bone saw. What followed was wild, absolutely wild, right up to the moment she blacked out.

"A cyst and a tumor," Brooks reported, trying not to tremble. "The tumor was tiny, and the surgeon feels sure he got it all, but they will biopsy it to be on the safe side. The cyst was large but filled with fluid, so it was drained and removed. At least as much as they could safely get, so a small shunt was put in just in case fluid builds in that area again. But that was after she stroked and they put her into the coma."

A gasp went around the room. Brooks rubbed a hand over his face and bowed his head. He still couldn't believe it. She'd never forgive him if she came out of this with serious impairment, even if they had saved her life—and that was if she understood all that had happened.

"She will come out of the coma, won't she?" Magnolia asked.

He nodded, trying desperately to believe it. "She should. The instant they realized what was happening, the anesthesiologist put her under and flooded her with drugs to stop the stroke, but it could be a while before she wakes up and only then will we really know what specific parts of her brain are affected. The neurologist thinks it could be very localized. They say, with all the pressure inside her head, it's a wonder she hasn't had a stroke before this."

"Well, that's something to be thankful for," Hub said, and Brooks nodded. He was thankful, even if it meant the end of all his personal hopes and dreams.

"Will you be staying here, then?" Morgan asked as they all began to gather their things.

Brooks nodded, but then he thought better of it. "For a while, but Ricky has to be my immediate priority." He turned to a very subdued Magnolia, saying, "I want to explain this to him myself, so if you could just tell him that his mom is resting comfortably, I'll be down to talk to him a little later."

Magnolia nodded, patted his shoulder and followed Hub, Odelia and Kent out. Brooks saw them on their way, then he slipped into Eva's ICU cubicle. She had been intubated, though he had no real idea if it was necessary. Better to be safe than sorry, though. Propped on her side, her caged head slightly elevated, she was surrounded by machines. He tried to take comfort in the readings, but the doctor in him held little sway over the man who stood in this darkened room.

He kissed her forehead, her cheek, her hands, which he kept in his as he bent over and whispered into her ear.

"I love you. I would do anything to help you, to make you well and whole. Please get well and come back to me. I need you. I don't know how I managed to this point without you. Your son and I both need you. I'll be praying for you. I love you."

He had no idea if she could hear him. Probably not. He felt better, stronger, for having said it, though. Now if only God would grant him the chance to tell her again when he knew she could hear and understand…

Chapter Fifteen

After speaking to the nurse and ascertaining that the doctor intended to keep Eva in the drug-induced coma for a period of at least twenty-four hours, Brooks changed and drove back to Buffalo Creek. Once there, he went straight to Chatam House.

Ricky was understandably distressed when Brooks explained the situation to him, so Brooks comforted them both by staying the night at Chatam House and sleeping in the extra room in the East Suite. He showed Ricky the papers he had signed, making him Ricky's guardian in the event his mother became unable to care for him.

"So I'd live with you if my mom doesn't get well?"

"Yes. *If* she doesn't get well," Brooks told him. "I'm not saying that's going to happen, but maybe you'd like to see my house on the way to school in the morning."

Ricky said he would, so they left early enough to swing by Brooks's place. It was a nice house that he'd had built only about six years ago, with a pretty pool and patio and a shady lawn, nothing too ostentatious but something in which a successful family doctor could take pride.

"Do you play billiards?" Brooks asked as they walked through the game room. Ricky shook his head. "I'll teach you. Play the piano?" Another head shake. "Maybe you'll want to take lessons sometime."

"Mom might want to," Ricky said hopefully.

Brooks smiled. She had to survive and retain enough dexterity and mental acuity for that. *Please, God,* he prayed. He'd been praying since the alarm had sounded in the operating room.

After he let Ricky out at school, he drove into Dallas to the hospital, but all he could do was pace, hold her hands and whisper to her. In midafternoon the neurologist came in to say that they would start gradually weaning her off the drugs that night and hope to awaken her enough to run some tests by the next morning. He suggested to Brooks that he go home and go about his business. Brooks remembered how many times he'd given that same advice, and laughed, though it wasn't in the least funny.

He drove back to Buffalo Creek in time to pick up Ricky from school. They shared dinner, and Brooks took Ricky to prayer meeting with him, where they prayed earnestly for his mom. Then they drove together into Dallas to see her. The breathing tube had been removed, and she was breathing comfortably on her own, which was a great relief, but she didn't wake or seem to know that they were there. Nevertheless, Brooks encouraged Ricky to tell his mom that he loved her and would see her the next day. Brooks whispered the same and kissed her good-night.

Once more he stayed at Chatam House, though he took Ricky with him to his house for fresh clothing first. Brooks refused to believe that one day soon Eva wouldn't join the two of them there. He had to believe it. He couldn't bear to believe anything else.

On Thursday he dropped Ricky off at school and drove back into Dallas. When he walked into the ICU cubicle and found it empty, he panicked. His doctor's brain knew that she was most likely awake and in a regular room somewhere, but the man who loved Eva Belle Russell only knew that she was not where he'd left her, and he went on a tear, demanding to know where she was and what was happening.

She had been assigned a room, but she was not there, as it happened. She was in the neurology lab undergoing tests, and this time nothing Brooks said or did got him entry. Furious, he called everyone from Murdock to the surgeon and anesthesiologist, but the newest doctor on the

ase, the neurologist, called the shots, and he had
ocked out Brooks. The reasons for it were no
doubt solid and numerous. The average family
member never got access, after all. Nevertheless,
Brooks did something he never did: he lost his
temper—which finally got him a meeting with
the neurologist.

"You've interrupted my work just to get a partial report!" the pale, insipid fellow sniffed.

"Is she fully conscious?" Brooks demanded.

"Yes."

"Motor skills?"

"Normal."

"Speech impairment?"

"None."

"Cognitive abilities?"

"So far so good," the fellow informed him.
The main problem seems to be memory."

Brooks's blood ran cold. "What has she forgotten?"

"That has not been fully determined yet, but
should have a very good idea within the next
hour or so."

Brooks checked his watch. "I have to go so I
can pick up my...her son from school."

"I'll leave the report in her room for you."

"Fair enough."

He wound up confessing his sin of anger as
he drove toward Buffalo Creek to pick up Ricky
from school, not even having glimpsed Eva. What

would he do if she had forgotten him? He would start over, woo her, win her heart, do whatever he had to do. He would fight for her, and he would keep on praying.

After picking up Ricky from school, Brooks called Chatam House to tell everyone there what he'd found out about Eva's condition while he and Ricky drove into Dallas. Again. For the first time, Brooks realized what families with patients in hospitals really went through, and he resolved to be more compassionate than he had before with the arrangements he made in the future. Having a loved one in the hospital, especially any distance from home, proved to be a traumatic experience for everyone involved.

He was shocked when he pushed through the door of Eva's room and found Morgan and Lyla there. Eva sat up in bed, a bright, welcoming smile on her face, despite the apparatus caging her head and keeping it still.

"Hi, there!" she sang out.

Relief shot through Brooks. "You know me?"

"Of course, I know you. You're the hunky doctor I love. I don't have a clue as to your name, but I know everything else about you."

He hadn't really heard anything since the word *love*, and his expression must have shown it because Morgan punched him in the arm and said "Tell her your name, stupid."

"Uh. Brooks L-Leland," he stuttered, dropping

Ricky's hand and moving mechanically toward the bed. "Brooks Harris Leland."

"Get down here and kiss me, Doc. Now that I am on the mend you are going to have to learn to toe the line, buster."

Smiling, he bent and placed both hands on the bed, one on either side of her. She'd filled out some over these past weeks, enough to add some lushness to her curves and make his heart race. Very carefully but quite thoroughly, he kissed her.

Afterward, he asked, "Do you recall me telling you that I love you?"

She frowned. "I seem to remember something about making it this far."

He kissed her again and said, "I love you."

She grinned and quipped, "I have witnesses, you know, and one of them is my handsome son." She crooked a finger at Ricky and said, "Come here, sugar, and tell me your name."

He looked confused for a moment, so Brooks explained that in some cases, stroke victims forgot the names of people they knew, even people they knew very well. They might remember everything else about a person but forget their names. They might also forget other things, but they would be things they could relearn.

"It is," he said, "no big deal in this case."

"Sweetie," she said to Ricky, "I didn't know my own name until they told me this morning."

Ricky's eyebrows jumped at that. "My name is

Ri—" He broke off and started again, glancing at Brooks. "My name is Richard Russell Allenson. The guys at school call me Rich."

She nodded. "I like it."

"It's because of the limo and Chatam House and everything," he confessed. "It used to be Ricky, but I like Rich best, and when you guys are married can I change my last name to Leland?"

Brooks imagined that Eva looked as stunned as he felt.

"Did you, um, ask me to marry you and I forget?" she quipped, rolling her eyes up at him.

"Nooo, but now that the matter's been raised..." He could hear Morgan snickering behind him and elbowed Ricky—er—Rich in the shoulder, muttering, "You could've waited until I bought a ring at least."

Ricky/Rich shrugged. Brooks sighed and picked up her hand in his.

"Eva Belle Russell," he began.

"That's me," she quipped, winking at everyone else in the room.

"Will you—"

"Whoa, whoa, whoa," she interrupted. "I refuse to be proposed to in a hospital bed. Besides, I can't remember the names of everyone I want to invite to the wedding right now."

Brooks bit his lip and bowed his head. "Noted."

She grinned and said, "And after this fiasco that rock better be worth the travail."

Brooks laughed. "I'll see what I can do."

Morgan started pounding him on the back then, and Lyla was telling Eva all about their hurried wedding, and *Rich* wanted to know how soon they could open the pool at *their* house. Brooks thought the kid would faint dead away from sheer delight when he told him the thing was heated. Then somehow they were all on their knees around that bed, thanking God.

No day could be more perfect for a proposal than Valentine's Day. Rich escorted his mom into the breakfast room where Brooks waited. The days since Eva's surgery had been busy ones. She was none too steady on her feet still, but she'd strapped on her red high heels, anyway, and made herself as presentable as possible, despite the bandage underneath her hair.

Chester had laid a fire, and the table was covered with crisp white linens. Music played via a system moved in from the family room. Eva had heard whispers about the selections to be played tonight, as well as the menu: Cornish hens, braised potatoes, asparagus. The whole Chatam family seemed to have had a hand in planning the event. They were lovely, although Eva still could not recall half their names. Brooks had assured her that remembering who was who was no small feat, even for those who *hadn't* suffered a stroke.

Brooks wore his good black suit, a white shirt

and a red tie, in keeping with the holiday theme; a big, heart-shaped box of chocolates was clutched in the crook of one arm and a bouquet of red roses in the other hand. He thrust the flowers at her, but she barely had time to sniff them before her son snatched them away and plunked them, wrapping and all, into a waiting vase of water. The chocolates came next. She admired the cellophane-wrapped box until Rich took it and placed it on the table. Then he gave her a quick hug, all but pushed her into a chair, winked at Brooks and hurried from the room.

Their secluded little table wasn't really secluded at all, as their friends, their *family*, waited in the dining room to celebrate what could only be a foregone conclusion. The silly man had to know that she loved him insanely, just as she knew, without a shadow of a doubt, that he loved her. Still, she treasured these romantic gestures more than she could say.

When he went down on one knee, she started to cry. She couldn't help it. She always cried when she was deliriously happy. Then he showed her the ring, and she had to joke because she always joked when she was appalled.

"Darling, why didn't you just mount the van in a platinum setting? I'll need armed guards if I try to wear that in public."

"You'll wear it and happily," he told her, sliding

he freakishly large diamond onto her finger. It
vas fabulous.

"Now, say you'll marry me."

"I'll marry you."

He got up, pulled her to her feet and kissed her,
ong and so well that they eventually drew ap-
plause, for the others had grown tired of waiting
or the announcement and had come to peek. They
urned together, arm in arm, to beam at their au-
dience. The aunties stood there in the front, smil-
ng benignly.

"There will be one more wedding to celebrate,"
aid Hypatia, back on her feet and beaming.

"Thanks to Chatam House," Brooks confirmed,
miling down at Eva.

"And the faith that fills it," she added, tilting
her head onto his shoulder.

"One more happy ending," Odelia trilled, clap-
ing her hands together so that her heart-shaped
earrings bounced above the pink-and-red ruffles
n her shoulders.

"But let the ending be a long time coming,"
offered Magnolia sagely.

"A very long time," Brooks promised.

"From your lips," Eva whispered, touching her
ingertip softly to those beloved features before
ifting her hand high, "to God's ears."

She no longer doubted that He heard or an-
wered in the way that was best for all concerned.
She understood so much now, and she finally

knew where and to whom she belonged. She knew right from wrong and good from bad and best from merely better—and where to find out what she didn't know. She looked at her son and saw his smile, and thanked God for what He had wrought from her foolishness.

On that thought, she bit her lip and waved her hand in front of her eyes, but it did no good. When the first sob broke through, the Chatams all gasped in dismay, but Brooks just gathered her gently against him, saying, "It's all right. She does this when she's happy."

Eva pointed a finger at Kent, wailing, "You, Money Bags, better invest in tissues, quick. I have the feeling I'm going to be d-doing this for the next thirty or forty y-years!"

They all laughed while she wept against Brooks's chest.

It could not have been more wonderful.

* * * * *

Dear Reader,

Have you ever been afraid to hope? The fear of failure, of not getting what we desperately want or need, can blunt our hope. Sometimes we give up rather than face the prospect of disappointment. Think of disappointing to the point of injury someone you love, the one person to whom you owe protection and consideration. That was the situation in which Eva Russell found herself: powerless, hopeless, desperate to protect the person who mattered most to her—only to find that others could matter, and hope has its own power when grounded in faith.

Aren't you glad that God is never powerless, that He is never without hope and never without purpose? Even when things don't work out just as we think they should, we can always trust that He is in control and has our best interests at heart. Now that gives me hope!

God bless,

Arlene James

LARGER-PRINT BOOKS!

GET 2 FREE LARGER-PRINT NOVELS PLUS 2 FREE MYSTERY GIFTS

Love Inspired

SUSPENSE
RIVETING INSPIRATIONAL ROMANCE

Larger-print novels are now available...

REQUEST YOUR FREE BOOKS!
2 FREE WHOLESOME ROMANCE NOVELS IN LARGER PRINT
PLUS 2
FREE
MYSTERY GIFTS

❊❊❊❊❊❊❊❊❊❊❊❊❊❊❊❊❊❊❊❊❊❊❊❊

HEARTWARMING™

❊❊❊❊❊❊❊❊❊❊❊❊❊❊❊❊❊❊❊❊❊❊❊❊

Wholesome, tender romances

YES! Please send me 2 FREE Harlequin® Heartwarming Larger-Print novels and my 2 FREE mystery gifts (gifts worth about $10). After receiving them, if I don't wish to receive any more books, I can return the shipping statement marked "cancel." If I don't cancel, I will receive 4 brand-new larger-print novels every month and be billed just $5.24 per book in the U.S. or $5.99 per book in Canada. That's a savings of at least 19% off the cover price. It's quite a bargain! Shipping and handling is just 50¢ per book in the U.S. and 75¢ per book in Canada.* I understand that accepting the 2 free books and gifts places me under no obligation to buy anything. I can always return a shipment and cancel at any time. Even if I never buy another book, the two free books and gifts are mine to keep forever.

161/361 IDN GHX2

Name _____ (PLEASE PRINT) _____

Address _____ Apt. # _____

City _____ State/Prov. _____ Zip/Postal Code _____

Signature (if under 18, a parent or guardian must sign)

Mail to the **Reader Service:**
IN U.S.A.: P.O. Box 1867, Buffalo, NY 14240-1867
IN CANADA: P.O. Box 609, Fort Erie, Ontario L2A 5X3

* Terms and prices subject to change without notice. Prices do not include applicable taxes. Sales tax applicable in N.Y. Canadian residents will be charged applicable taxes. Offer not valid in Quebec. This offer is limited to one order per household. Not valid for current subscribers to Harlequin Heartwarming larger-print books. All orders subject to credit approval. Credit or debit balances in a customer's account(s) may be offset by any other outstanding balance owed by or to the customer. Please allow 4 to 6 weeks for delivery. Offer available while quantities last.

Your Privacy—The Reader Service is committed to protecting your privacy. Our Privacy Policy is available online at www.ReaderService.com or upon request from the Reader Service.

We make a portion of our mailing list available to reputable third parties that offer products we believe may interest you. If you prefer that we not exchange your name with third parties, or if you wish to clarify or modify your communication preferences, please visit us at www.ReaderService.com/consumerschoice or write to us at Reader Service Preference Service, P.O. Box 9062, Buffalo, NY 14240-9062. Include your complete name and address.

HW15